Be Careful What You Witch For

Enchantress Chronicles, Volume 1

Fiona West

Published by Fiona West, 2024.

For my amazing children:

There's nothing I wouldn't do for you. I love you to
the moon and back.

TABLE OF CONTENTS

MAP

MADAME MONTANGE
LE SOMMET SOLITAIRE
RENAULT AND ALYA'S JOURNEY
L'AUBERGE DU HIBOU
HAGUENAU
REFUGE DU TRAPPEUR
SAINTE-ANNE
ARC ET FLÉCHE
CREUX DE SAINETTE
PONT DES CERFS
BEAUCHAMP

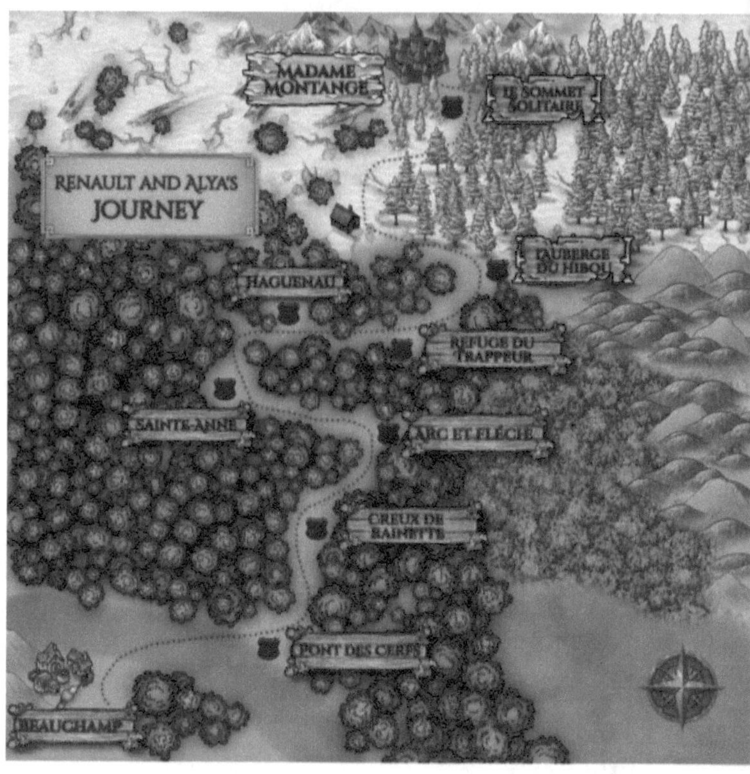

AUTHOR'S NOTE

One reason we read is to experience things that mean something. It's not very compelling to just hear about a character's day through the lens of normality: the cereal she ate, how she got mustard on her blouse, the traffic she sat in on the way home. No, we read to find out what's at stake: is she eating that cereal to lose weight or lower her cholesterol, or is it her favorite from childhood, soaked in more sugar than any human needs in a full day? Did the mustard mean she blew the big meeting, or was it a funny thing she laughed about later with a guy in line at the coffee shop? Was it in the shape of Michigan, reminding her of that canoe trip she took with her dad in middle school when he told her she was adopted? Sitting in traffic, did she listen to a podcast that made her cry? Did she rear-end someone and feel that sick, sinking feeling that usually accompanies your insurance going up? We don't just want to know what happens; we want to know what it means. (Hang on, I need to get a kid in the tub.)

We read for emotion, the inner life. But as a writer, when it's *your* inner life, putting it on display can be frankly terrifying.

I've written eighteen books now. Each one of them carries vital pieces of me: my chronic illness journey toward getting a diagnosis, the complexities of living in a foreign country, the deep rightness of falling in love with someone who sees your soul and says, "Yeah. I feel that, too." But until now, my parenting journey has mostly stayed off the page. (The bath water is not yet running, for anyone keeping score.) The one exception was a small-town romance about a librarian who's getting divorced. Though I am happily married for nearly twenty years now, I tried to relay how stretched thin she felt, how frayed and utterly transparent, when it came to parenting. And mostly, I get two kinds of reviews: some that praise the honesty, and others that recommend counseling for me and my characters. Both are probably fair, but neither was my goal. Because we also read to be seen. I've wanted that since the first time I read *Dealing with Dragons* by Patricia C. Wrede, where the princess was not only a brunette like me, but preferred fencing to cross-stitch and deigned to run off with dragons rather than marrying a stranger.

I have debated about whether to publish this book so many times, I've lost count. It is intensely personal in a new way, a more vulnerable way. Parenting a neurodiverse child as a neurodiverse adult is gonna get messy–there's no way around it. Yet I know I'm not alone in this–most of us would admit there have been times in our parenting when we just look at our partner and laugh. (I just called to my kid, who was making up stories in the mirror instead of getting into the bath. Water's still off.) It's either laugh or cry, right? We do our fair share of both. There's nothing as humbling as being completely baffled by someone *you made* who looks up at you with eyes like your mother's and hair like your sister's and refuses to do anything you ask for. (Update: there is a claim that the tub stopper is broken. Partner is investigating.)

But ultimately, this story wants to be told. Not because everyone in it is perfect or even always likable, but because it's a testament to what it means to be strong, and it's not being stoic or solitary. It's my treatise on navigating the stormy waters of diagnosis and difference, of well-meant advice that does nothing at all and pockets of help in the least likely places. (The water is running. Hallelujah.)

In example, I paused writing this article here to read my oldest child a few chapters in *The Restaurant at the End of the Universe* by Douglas Adams, a tome some of you towel-carriers may be familiar with, and it was unexpectedly helpful. (During this time, I also made up and performed a song about how my youngest child should actually get *in* the tub, now that it is full; it had a great beat, but the rhymes were lacking, despite "ub" being a very common phoneme. The response was understandably tepid...much like the bath water, I assume.) I tell you this because aside from our abnormal kid experiences, there are many normal ones, too. The mundane and the mysterious mix in daily life to the point where it can lose meaning sometimes, unless we really stop to think about it.

But back to the helpful book: we read the part where Zaphod Beeblebrox, the two-headed former president of the Galaxy, having survived a failed assassination attempt, is then forced to get into a device called the Total Perspective Vortex. In case you are picturing something sinister rather than silly, it runs partially on fairy cake and merely steals your soul by showing you the entire universe all at once...and then putting the tiniest dot imaginable where you are, the thought being that if you really, really understood how insignificant your corner of the universe is, while galaxies upon galaxies spin and supernovas go critical and new stars are born, you wouldn't be able to handle it.

The story Zaphod tells himself is that he's the center of the universe and therefore apt to have things work out for him, and he survives. But the story I tell myself is that the center of the universe is rather irrelevant if my small corner of it can be filled with love and acceptance and support for experiences that are outside the norm, and that is how I survive. Deep is my love for Mr. Adams' work, but I don't think knowing how infinitesimally small I am compared to the rest of the universe is what would break me. In fact, small things are what matters most, and the closer I am to them, the closer I am to being happy.

This book is one of those small things. It is not literature by any measure and it won't be remembered decades from now like Mr. Adams, nor will it make sense to everyone. But to those it does, I hope it makes you feel seen as you make your own way through dark forests or vast galaxies, knowing that you are not alone.

And now, if you'll excuse me, I have a child to remove from the bath...

CHAPTER ONE

Valerie

By the time Renault comes back with the witch, Alya has smashed two ceramic soup bowls against the wood floor and is working to strip the sheets from the bunk beds. The light-haired woman stares at my daughter, her steps slowing as she reaches the middle of the common room, the firelight flickering over her snow-white skin.

"Mama," my youngest whimpers, and I open my arms to her. From her hiding place under the kitchen table with her sisters, Fayette flies to me and latches onto my waist like a white-striped twigjumper. She's never been comfortable around the magic users, but we have no choice. Strange that her sister's temper frightens her less than Jeanette, a middle-aged woman who reminds me of my aunt.

"Are you all right?" Renault asks, his voice low in my ear. I nod. It's a lie. I am so far from that state, I can't even speak. Our precious girl, once again out of control, and

I'm powerless to help her.

"No one understands!" Alya screams, her voice bouncing off the log walls. She's trying to rip the sheets with her bare hands, but eight years of life have not given her enough strength to do so, thank Woz. "No one loves me! None of you! You're ruining my life!"

"Cherie," Jeanette says softly. At that endearment, Alya turns to look at her for the first time, chest heaving, angry tears still streaming down her face.

"Valerie, take the children outside," Renault murmurs, but I shake my head. I will stay this time. I will not leave her alone with another stranger. I need her to believe that while her first statement may be the truth—I *don't* understand her—her second is not. My heart is for her, whatever she may think. I pass Fayette into his arms, as if to say *Take them if you want to.*

"Why do you rage, little one?" the witch asks.

"Val," Renault repeats insistently, but I ignore him. *You married a nightstallion of a woman, Renault. You knew that. You could've had petite Léa or pretty Sylvia, but you chose the black-smith's daughter. You knew the steel of me.*

"No one understands," Alya repeats, but the storm in her is waning. My heart falls; if the witch cannot see the full effect, will she still be able to help us?

I needn't have worried. Alya kicks at a fragment of the bowl, sending it flying toward us. The witch stops it in the air with a lifted hand.

"Do you want to hurt your family?" the witch asks, and Alya's temper ignites again.

"This isn't my *family*," she shouts. "A family loves you. A family respects you! A family does not work you like a slave." Her voice rings off the low eaves, the small room bursting with her anger.

The witch pivots to me. "What did you ask of her?"

"I asked her to wash the soup bowls. Just the bowls, not even the pot or the spoons." The offense in it still mystifies me, but it is always like this. The tiniest request prompts a hurricane. She doesn't send the storm, not really. The rest of the time, she's my clever, silly girl who loves hugs and kisses and playing with her sisters, and I know deep down that she's not *choosing* this. But I am tired of having us both shipwrecked on the rocks of this affliction, inside and out. I am so tired. My gaze goes to the window; it's dark now. She won't try to run away; she fears the forest at night, like the other girls.

Alya slumps into a chair and puts her head in her hands with a sob. Slowly, I pick my way through the sharp shards to her. I put my hand on her blonde head, feeling my own lower lip tremble. Even though she's four years older than Fayette, she turns and buries her face in my skirts, wrapping her arms around me like a vise, her body shaking. I rub her back in big, slow circles. Behind me, Renault and the witch are speaking in low tones.

"Mama." My heart pangs that Alya's voice is hoarse from her exertions. "I'm hungry."

The storm is over. There is still the aftermath, but the worst is done. Her sisters know it, too; I can hear them crawling out from under the table. I cross carefully back to the kitchen and find her some soft cheese with herbs in it, the kind she likes, with a little crusty bread.

"Thank you, Mama," Alya says with a watery smile. "Have you seen my paper dolls?"

She's all sunshine or all storm in the blink of an eye. It somehow exhausts me even more.

"I do," Margot pipes up, and I give her a grateful pat on the head as she leads the girls into the closet. Even Fayette wriggles from my husband's arms to scramble after them. *So forgiving.* I would like to think I've taught them that, but I don't know.

Perhaps children are just more ready to forget, more ready to embrace.

"Is it always like that?" the witch asks as Renault offers her a chair.

"Sometimes worse," I say, relieved that I have found my voice again.

"How often?"

Renault speaks up. "Every day. Or nearly that. She is bankrupting us with broken pottery. I know many children say such things to their parents in a temper, but not daily, and she's threatened harm to herself."

I peek into our bedroom; Alya is giving Clothilde a bite of her snack.

"And you have spoken to the priest?"

I nod. "He says it's not spiritual. He recommended a firmer hand with her."

Renault grunts discontentedly, and the witch raises an eyebrow.

"He recommended we paddle her," I admit. "We tried it briefly. It didn't help." *And I hated it every time. It went against my every instinct.*

"Only made things worse," my husband agrees.

"And the doctor?"

"The one in town, Monsieur Garnier, did not know of any affliction that might do this."

The witch sighed. "Well, it's not magic. It was nervous around her, sensing the emotions, but it wasn't interacting with her at all. I'd have been able to feel that. And I don't see any marks of a curse."

Tears burn behind my eyes, but I won't let them fall. I don't know why it's so disappointing; I didn't think it was magic. I didn't want it to be. I just...wanted an answer. Wanted help. The girls could come back in at any moment. I will save my tears for tonight, tucked in bed, with Renault like a wall behind me, his big arms wrapped tight around me. *Stay closed. Stay shut down. Just for now.*

"There is another person we haven't considered: Madame Montagne. She specializes in many things. I have sent families to her before, and many came back helped."

"But isn't she expensive?" I ask, twisting the edge of my apron.

"Not always. It may be that you have something else she would want."

"A Favor," Renault murmurs, and a shudder goes through me when the witch nods. I have always avoided magical debt, but for Alya...for her, I would do it. That and more. What else can we do? This was our last resort, and it has failed.

"The journey is far, though," Jeanette says. "You'll be three weeks gone, all told."

"We can't take them all with us," I whisper to Renault, and he just looks at me sadly. "And what about the animals? We can't..."

"Thank you for your time," he says to the witch, getting to his feet and offering his hand. That's what I realize—I can't go, either. We'll be separated for all that time. I'm still trying to wrap my mind around the idea as he pays her at the door and wishes her a safe journey home. He sits back down next to me, and I take his hand, twisting our fingers together, tipping to rest my forehead on his shoulder.

"What can we do?" I feel his voice rumble through his bones.

"If we do nothing, nothing will change."

"Or it may get worse."

I sit up, wiping tears I hadn't held back after all. "I can't handle that."

"So I say again, what are our options?"

I reach out and stroke his dark beard, sprinkled with gray like dandelion seeds. "You should take her and go. We'll sell Milkrose. I think she's pregnant. We'll get a good price; it will be enough to cover the journey." *But not Madame Montagne's Favor.*

He scowls. "What will you do for milk, then? The goat doesn't give enough..."

"We have cheese. Maybe someone needs help with washing..."

"You're stretched too thin already, and it'll be worse when I'm gone. We can't—"

"Renault, please." My voice breaks, and I put a hand over my mouth to try to take the sound back. His face softens, and he pulls me into his embrace. The smell of crawlergourd ale and woodsmoke on him steadies me, and the words come easier. "She's our daughter. We have to help her. We have to prove her wrong. Every day, she claims we don't care about her, and I couldn't tell you why, but she believes it with everything she is. I know her words are strange, too old for such a young child. But my heart is in pieces over it, and every day, she smashes them again. We have to show her that we love her, to prove it beyond doubt in her mind. We have to."

"I know," he says, squeezing me tighter. "You're right. Of course you're right."

Fayette wanders in then, and I quickly wipe my cheeks. "Yes, cherie?"

The way she's rubbing her eyes tells me what she wants; it's been a long day. I lift her into my arms so she doesn't cut her feet and start the kettle for her bath. Renault will sweep while I bathe them, and soon, it'll be like it never happened. Only it did happen, and it will happen again. Beyond Renault's love, it is the only thing I'm sure of.

They bathe as children do, with silly bubble beards and flicked splashes and happy shrieks, the rest of the evening already forgotten. But I know they're exhausted when Clothilde and Fayette fall asleep before I've finished *The Cat Who Caught the Moon,* one of their favorites. I kiss Margot, on the top bunk, still reading her own book in the dim firelight, and she gives me a smile.

When I kneel next to Alya, I tuck the covers tighter around her, because she likes the feeling. *I do know you, darling,* I want to tell her. *I know you won't touch steamed leaflets, and I know you hate the feel of stiff church dresses around your neck. I know you could recite all our bedtime stories by heart. I'm paying attention; I promise I am. I'm sorry I haven't figured this out yet. I am trying. Please believe me.*

"You're going on a trip soon," I tell her with as big of a smile as I can muster, but she picks up on my words.

"With you?"

"No, just Papa."

Her scowl is fierce. "What? Why? We've always traveled together. Always." And even that has been few and far between.

I haven't spent more than a day away from this man since we married. There was simply no reason to, and the farm needed us.

"Not this time." I kiss the top of her head, lingering a bit longer than I did with the rest of them. "You're going to see a friend of ours. Someone who can help."

Her eyebrows dance in confusion. "Help with what?"

The words catch in my throat. "Never mind. Sweet dreams, cherie."

Two days later, the whole family comes out front to see them off. Alya's cloudy breath mingles with the horse's as I help her up in front of Renault.

"I wish you could come, too," she pouts, and I try to give her a smile.

"Me too. Be good for Papa." It's so deeply wrong how thankful I am to have a break from her, and the guilt of it cuts me like a new hunting knife.

"Send me a letter everywhere you stop," I tell Renault sternly, and he gives me a grin, even though I can tell he's hurting, too.

"Just don't let the children see their content," he replies, giving me a mischievous look. I whack his leg, and the horse thinks I'm prompting her and lurches forward. The other girls wave with me. But by the time the horse disappears around the bend in the road, I'm alone in the yard. There are chickens that need feeding and dishes that need washing from our hasty breakfast. It's accomplishing nothing, watching the empty road. It doesn't even make me feel better. But standing there, I send my heart after them.

CHAPTER TWO

Renault

"Papa."

"Urmg."

"Papa." Someone's small hand is shaking my shoulder gently. "Papa, I want breakfast."

"Valerie…" I mumble, reaching for my wife, but the bed next to me is empty. I open my eyes and look around. *Right. Another inn.* Another day on the road with my daughter awaits me. The child sleeps like an angry rock marten in our shared bed, burrowing in the sheets and thrashing and talking as she dreams.

"She's not here, Papa," Alya explains patiently, as she has for the last two days. "And I'm hungry."

"Right," I say, forcing myself upright, rubbing the remnants of a poor night's sleep from my eyes. "Give me a minute and we'll go see what the offerings are."

Alya bounces with excitement, and I cringe; it's barely light. I scoop her up and plop her on the bed, tickling her lightly. At least laughter is a better wake-up call than the thump of her jumping feet for the people around us.

"Shh, little bird. We have to be quiet, remember?"

"I forgot," she giggles. She bounces on the bed instead, so I try to stay close by as I change out of my nightshirt into clean trousers and pray the frame doesn't break.

I miss Valerie. Not just because she gets up with the children, but I miss the scent of her on my pillow and the warmth of her in the morning...and at night.

She wasn't one of the girls who frequently gathered around the gate, wanting to buy eggs from me, when I moved to Beauchamp as a bachelor. Their pretty wicker baskets, their hair-tossing, and their tittering any time I said anything even remotely amusing made going to the gate something I dreaded. No, Valerie never came to the gate. But her mother did.

"You're new in town, yes?" Albertine seemed to assess me every time she came, but no time more than that first one.

"Yes. I just moved here from La Vallée des Regrets."

"Ah." Here, most of the women started asking why I'd left, where my wife was, and all sorts of other nosy questions I couldn't abide. But Albertine just lifted an eyebrow and looked down at my girls.

"I ask because of your hens. I have not seen their like around here."

I launched into the kind of explanation Valerie chides me for now—*no one wants so much information about the hens, cherie. Just make it less. Not so much*—but she was not there then to stop me, and Albertine smiled, nodding, listening, asking a few questions. She bought ten speckled eggs and left. It was the most pleasant interaction I'd had in days.

When she returned the next week, I mentioned I hadn't yet gotten a haircut since I came to town. Several of the gate women had commented on it, touching my prematurely gray locks before I pushed their hands away gently, despite my annoyance.

"I'll take you to Feline, if you like. She's my sister's girl. She'll give you a good price."

"I'd appreciate that, thank you." Since I wasn't familiar with Feline's house, she offered to walk me there. The dust from our feet and passing horses floated up, exposed in the slanted sunshine, and I marveled again at the beauty of the place, still so new to me. The quivering birches and little mossy streams were enchanting, and every cottage seemed to have a thatched roof growing seeds that squirrels had buried, but no one minded. Away from the road, the thicker forest of pine and cedar made a house of their own, but still the nutbushes and ferns managed somehow in the thin light. My uncle's family seemed fools to have left, but I couldn't help but be grateful they had.

We passed through the middle of town, and the scent of fruit in the sun wafted to us. Fallen cherries, late peaches and early apples. I was watching for cranberries; I love them dried in the wintertime. The butcher's wife was out, waving off the flies from her products with a once-white apron, and I angled away from two of my gate women who were buying a roast.

The farrier was working on a horse's shoe; their smell was less nice than the fruit, but it was still an honest smell. Animals are rarely capable of falsehood, and I admired them for it. Smoke billowed from the blacksmith's chimney, and a huge dark-haired man with a big beard was working at the anvil on a plow blade that needed repairing.

"That's my Gaël," she said, waving. And the man stopped to wave back, then came over to the fence.

"Is this our egg man?"

"That's right," she said, and I shook his hand.

"Best omelet I ever had," he said, nodding at the memory. "I don't know how you get the yolks so bright yellow."

"Good nutrition. It's simple, really."

"Well, it was delicious. My compliments, truly."

I shifted my weight from foot to foot, uncomfortable under the man's sincere praise. That's when Valerie came out of the forge, her face smudged with dark dirt the same color as her raven locks.

"Papa, are you done? I need to go home in case Guylaine comes by with more wool." She ignored me completely, which was strange, because if I saw a man whose soul had left his body, I think I'd notice. She was the most beautiful person I'd ever seen.

"Come over and say hello to the egg man," Gaël prompted, and her lips went flat with apparent displeasure. But she did as he asked, picking her away across the yard littered with bent metal and various hammers, her hand extended. The gate women wanted me to kiss the back of their hands, but not this one. Not Valerie. She gave me a firm handshake, then turned back to her mother, who licked her thumb before she attempted to clean her face. My dark-haired angel squirmed away, shaking the dust and soot off her skirts.

"Go wash your face, and you can walk with us. Renault and I are headed that way as well."

"Very well." She turned on her heel and headed back toward the stone building. I won't say it damaged my ego to have her dismiss me so out of hand, but it was certainly not my typical experience, and I took note.

"And who was that?" I asked as we waited for her by the slatted wood fence.

"Oh!" Albertine laughed. "We didn't introduce you, did we? My apologies. That's our Valerie. She doesn't much care for people. Books are her main interest, weapons somewhat less than books, but still more than people."

"I like her already." The words flew from my mouth before I could stop them, and my cheeks pinked as Albertine and Gaël laughed.

"Yes, she is like you, I think," Albertine agreed. "You prefer a simple life, uncomplicated. Unencumbered."

"I don't mind being involved with others, as long as the expectations are clear." The couple exchanged a look I couldn't interpret.

"You know, I forgot to start my bread for tonight, so I'll have to go to the bakery; would you mind if Valerie showed you the way? She can show you as well as I can, if she's going that way, regardless."

I hesitated. If I was seen walking through town with a young woman, was it going to bring *more* women to my gate? I needed the business, but not the irritation. Still, I did need a haircut. Albertine would take me if I asked, but why would I make her? She'd been so kind to me. And she was a customer. I shouldn't put her to any trouble for my sake.

"That would be fine."

"You had to think about it a long time," Gaël rumbled, raising an eyebrow in my direction, but Albertine shushed him.

"Careful consideration is a wonderful quality. Here she comes now."

She'd tied her hair back in a simple style and cleaned up her skin except for a smudge on her forearm that I noticed as she unlatched the front gate. I smiled, and she just stared at me.

"Could you please show Renault the way to Feline's? I have some things to do in town."

"Of course. Come on." She started down the road without waiting to see if I was following, and I hurried to catch her. Her strides were as long as mine, and I fell into step next to her as we continued through town. There weren't many stalls or shops left, and soon, we were beneath the trees again.

"Is it far?"

"No. Just a bit past our place."

That surprised me. "You don't live in town?"

Her quick smile was there and gone before I'd appreciated its beauty as much as I wanted to. "No, Papa thinks it's better to breathe fresh air and fall asleep with the creek lulling us. He doesn't like the hustle and bustle."

"I'm with him on that one."

"You live on Monsieur Cartier's old property, don't you?"

I nod. "He was my uncle, my mother's brother. When he died, he left it to me."

"And you raise chickens? Is that lucrative?"

My heart sank a little. Was this conversation moving toward my eligibility to marry? I wouldn't mind just making a friend, and I certainly needed no more hassle at the gate.

"I do all right."

"Have you tried feeding them shell fragments? I read it would increase their egg output and strengthen the shells of the new."

I turned my head slowly to look at her. "You read about chickens?"

She shrugged. "Nothing else to read that day. You can read fairy tales only so many times."

I thought about this and found I agreed, though I wasn't sure it was a popular opinion.

"The chickens don't dislike it? I think it would disgust me if I were them."

She laughed. "You don't like the idea of consuming something that came from you?"

I screwed up my face. "No."

Valerie laughed again. "You're likely not alone in that. But no, they don't mind. You should try it, see if you can continue to make your enterprise more profitable." She stopped by a gate, and I stopped with her. I would've followed her much, much farther, and I couldn't actually remember why I was following her in the first place. That's how I should've known I was infatuated.

"Well? Aren't you going inside?"

"Oh! Yes. Could you perhaps introduce us? I don't want your cousin thinking a stranger is breaking into her yard."

Valerie smirked at me. "My cousin is fairly unflappable, but as you wish."

She wasn't wrong. Feline was kind and had the same force of character as the rest of her family, and the haircut she gave me was serviceable. Valerie sat and chatted with us while she worked, waiting for her to finish before parting ways with us, which I appreciated. As I walked home that day, rubbing at my short hair, I thought about what excuse I could come up with to see her again. Uncle's farm was old; surely there was some piece of broken equipment I could bring to Gaël to fix. But as it happened, I didn't need to.

When I went out to the gate the next morning, Valerie was waiting, her mother's basket over her arm.

"Is everything all right with your mother?" I asked with concern, hurrying as well as I could without jostling the eggs too much.

Valerie's smile was bright. "She's fine. I just volunteered. My father was in the mood for custard tonight, and we thought your eggs would make the best ingredient."

"They will," I said, picking out the best ones for her. "I've made it myself. It's excellent."

We chatted—I can't remember about what now, but when I went back inside, I'd spent the better part of an hour out there with her. The next time, I invited her inside for a croissant. She returned the favor and invited me to their house for lemon cake, made with my eggs. But I didn't kiss her until several months later, after I asked her father if I could marry her. Those lips would be mine and mine alone.

"You're getting married?" Sylvia was one of my most consistent gate women, touching my arm and laughing nasally too often. Today, though, there was no flirting in her, just anger.

"Yes." I held out the basket so she could choose, but she didn't.

"What do you want with her? She's strange. Everyone says so."

"I don't care much for public opinion."

"You never even called on me," the woman whined. "You didn't give me a chance. My papa has money, land. You would own it all. He has no male heirs."

"Then he ought to give it to *you*. How do you not see that?" I've never been good at smooth, calming words, and by the widening of her eyes, Sylvia had just realized that for the first time. But she should have found the injustice more galling than my honesty. I shook the basket insistently, clacking the eggs together dangerously, and she finally chose the ones she wanted.

"You'll regret it," she promised as she left. "You'll be an outcast with her in your house."

The inn has a nice breakfast, as it turns out. Alya crunches happily on crisp bacon, wiggling her backside in the worn wooden
chair as I write to Valerie.

Beloved,

*Could you, do you think, send your response on to the
inn farther down on our journey? I am hungry to hear
your words, to know how you are. Even if I missed it
on my way up, I could receive it on my way back. Please
let me know if the children are being good. There's no
carrier here, so I don't know when this letter will reach
you. I hate that. I take comfort in the fact that your
family is nearby if you need them, but they have their
own responsibilities, and every day, I think I should've
brought all of you with me.*

*I already miss holding you. I miss your sharp mind
and your wit. I miss listening to you read to our
daughters. You're a good mama. I'm sure you're tired;*

please try to rest and take some time for you as well, as I am not there to take the broom away from you. Take the children to your mother if you need a break. She'll be thrilled. I miss your quiet. I even miss our arguments. And I definitely miss the making up afterward...

Do you know, when I asked you to marry me, Sylvia told me I'd regret it? The gall of her. It's no wonder she ran off with that soldier. I'm so glad I didn't listen to her. We will get through this, beloved. You and me. Even though we're not together, you are in my heart and on my mind.

Give my love to the hens. And to our children.

Love,

Renault

CHAPTER THREE

Alya

Papa is writing another letter. It's his favorite thing to do when we stop. The rest of the day, he tries to bore me out of my mind by talking to me on the road. This inn looks much like the last one, except it has more dead animal heads looking down at me. I don't like the way the deer is staring. He looks angry. And it smells funny in here, like Papa's clothes when he's been working in the sun, left under the bed too long.

"Papa."

"Mmm?"

"How much farther is it to where we're going?" I'm guessing it's one day, but I hope it's less.

"Much farther, little bird," he says. "Can you try the eggs, please?"

Bacon is better than eggs. These are runny and strange—with *pocket parsley* and *squitchweed* of all things. I poke at them with my fork as he watches, but there's no way I'm putting that in my mouth.

"How much farther?" I ask again. "Two days?"

"Farther," he says, his ink pen still scratching over the rough paper. He seemed unhappy that it was the best the clerk had. Farther? We've been on the road three days already—whenever he goes to the market in Prairie Agréable, he's only gone one night.

"How will Mama get your letter anyway?"

He gestures to the stables out the window we're sitting next to. "A rider will carry this one. Once we get farther, the homegoer birds will carry it. There's one who knows the way to Beauchamp, and they'll release him."

"Magic?" I ask, trying not to sound too interested.

"No," he says with a smile, "just nature. These birds remember the place they're from."

"Mmm." I still want to know how far we're going, but I know he won't tell me. My whispers want to know, too. They whisper Mama's name, wondering where she is. They whisper about my sisters. I can't whisper back with Papa around, so we haven't talked much—just when I squat in the woods. They sound...fainter here. At home, they're loud—sometimes so loud, I get annoyed about it, wishing I could shoo them away like Fayette when I'm trying to read. But the magic here is quieter, and I wish I knew why. I don't even know for sure if that's what it is, just that they've always spoken to me since I knew what a word was. Jeanette the witch said it's not magic, but I don't think she could hear them. She used her hands.

"Who's collecting the eggs while you're gone?"

"Your mother will. Did you try *these* eggs?"

"Not Margot?" I press. He didn't want to let me do it when I asked. He said I'd break them. Gave me the *blah blah* about how the eggs were our family's livelihood and if I wasn't going to do the tasks I was asked to, I couldn't choose another one. That I wasn't responsible. Those words burned me like the woodstove. He doesn't understand. He never will.

"No, your mother. Try them, and we can share a swirlbark roll."

I DON'T WANT TO TRY THEM, I want to yell, but I promised Mama I'd be good.

"No."

Papa sighs, pulling my plate toward him to eat them himself. "All right, finish up that bacon, then. The sooner we get on the road, the better."

He doesn't understand, my papa. It isn't that I just hate being told what to do—I can't explain it, but it's worse than that. It's like a thousand voices screaming no. It's like I'm being locked up in chains and need to get free. My heart beats harder. I feel *scared*. He acts like it's easy, just following along with him, but it's not. It's *work*, and I'm trying. But the idea that I might see something new on the road puts my feet to movement, slowly, still dragging. At least I'll get away from that dead deer and the stink. At least we'll get where we're going.

CHAPTER FOUR

Valerie

I have just finished my kneading and set the bread to rise by the woodstove when the knock comes at the gate. I cast a glance at the grandfather clock, ticking serenely in the corner; it's too early for the children to be home from school, and my egg customers usually come much earlier. *If Clothilde has spilled that inkpot on herself again...* Wiping my hands on my apron, I stick my head out the top of the front door. A man I don't recognize stands at the gate, tapping an ebony cane against the sun-bleached wood. His maroon wool overcoat and green cap don't seem like something anyone I know would wear. Renault told me firmly to refuse any strangers while he was away, but I'm fairly sure he knew I was going to ignore that edict.

With light steps, I check on Fayette. She's still sleeping deeply on my bed, snuggled under the down comforter with a persistent winter sun trying to warm her through the window. Then I gather my boots, my sheepsweave wrap, and the egg basket. He turns before I make it all the way there.

"Ah, I was beginning to think you were out! Good morning, madame." He extends a hand. "I am Philippe Cartier; your husband is a cousin of mine."

Since the gate is still firmly shut, I take his hand and squeeze it in greeting. "It's nice to meet you, Monsieur Cartier, but I'm afraid you must be mistaken. My husband has no

29

cousin." I have been informed by my mother many times that I am overly suspicious of strangers due to reading too many suspenseful tales, but at moments like this, I do not regret a page of it. This man's hands seem too smooth and beautiful to be related to my Renault, the backs of whose hands are marked by scratching chickens and dark hair, freckled from too much sun. I know them like I know every divot and knot in our kitchen floor. And he still has not said my husband's name.

"Ah, yes," the man replies easily. "He thought me dead. I was recruited for an errand by the duke of our province, and I was sadly taken prisoner. But when I was ransomed, I completed the errand to his excellency's satisfaction, and *voila!* Here I am today, a rich man, as you can see." He's peering past me now toward the house, and it has the hair on the back of my neck standing up. "Is he at home?"

"Who?" I ask innocently. "The duke?"

"No, madame," he laughs. "Your husband. Renault." So he does know his name. But that means nothing—he could have gotten it from anyone in town.

"I'm afraid he's sick in bed and can't receive visitors. Where are you staying, cousin?" This is a gamble, since he won't be back for more than two weeks at the earliest...but I'm not ready to reveal my situation. Not to this man.

His frown makes him seem truly disappointed. "Well, I had hoped to stay here in my childhood home, but I don't want to impose if he's ill. What an unfortunate turn of events."

"Indeed," I agree, straight-faced. "But there's a woman in town who rents rooms: Madame Tortouf. Her home is across from the butcher. Perhaps you'd find it to your liking."

"Perhaps," he says, but his gaze is on my house again. *My home.* And it mimics perfectly the way Poppy looks at the bucket of oats in the morning, knowing it's for her. *Why do I miss a horse? So silly.*

"Would you give him a message for me, my dear? Would you tell him Philippe needs to speak with him as soon as he's well? It is a matter of some importance."

"Certainly, cousin. Good day to you. Take a few eggs for your breakfast tomorrow, if you'd like."

He seems amused by my offer. In fact, he's lucky I have any left; I'm usually sold out before the midday meal. But he makes a show of oohing and aahing over them, not realizing that he's praising Renault's work, not mine. I give him a faux smile, and he leaves with three speckled brown eggs.

It's after supper when I finally sit down to reply to my love's latest letter.

Dearest Renault,

I am sending this farther along your route, as you suggested, so I hope it gets to you. Your letter made me smile; I can just imagine you two spending your mornings together in a strange place. You, of course, have more experience with strange places than I do, being an Elsewherer from a foreign place like La Vallée des Regrets...I used to laugh when the girls in town would gossip about how exotic you were. It turns out even exotic men snore after too much beer. I hope you are able to enjoy the journey a little. You did not say whether

Alya is behaving herself, and I hope that means she is.
I'm praying for you every time I think of you.

"Mama, how do you spell 'disappointed'?" Margot asks at my elbow. I tell her as I stare into the dying fire, too tired to get up and stoke it again. I'll have to cut more wood tomorrow unless my father comes by to check on us. The thought of who else might come by makes my stomach churn uneasily.

"What are you writing, cherie?" I lean over to look and I'm somewhat surprised.

My father took my sister and went on a long journey.
I miss them both. I don't know when he will be back. I
am worried about them and disappointed I didn't get
to go. I want to see

I dip my head to see her better and tuck a wisp of dark hair behind her ear. "What did you wish to see?"

"Everything. Papa's valley. The mountains. And..." She hesitates, and her voice drops to a whisper. "The ocean." I don't have the same wanderlust as these two—my own village has been good enough. But the way she whispers it makes me wonder what I'm missing out on, like a secret.

"Papa wasn't going that way; he went north to the mountains. The ocean, that's a very long way."

"I wouldn't mind. I would bring a book."

I can't help but laugh, and I kiss her forehead. "I believe you will see it someday. Now finish quickly, and let's get the little ones into bed."

The girls are well. Clothilde started school and likes it fine. Her teacher says she is quiet and well-behaved, but that won't last long. We went to my mother's for dinner on Seventh Day and it was a pleasant change of pace.

But nothing is right without you. I forgot how much I hate shoveling dung. All your work and mine together is heavy, but even if you couldn't work beside me, I just feel lighter to talk with you, to hold you in the dark, avoiding going to sleep. Telling each other stories we both already know by heart.

And I tell myself that my eyes are too fatigued to write more in the dim light, that I ought to save the oil for Margot's schoolwork, not my own selfish pleasures. The girls need me to sing them to sleep; that's why the letter stops there with no mention of the rich cousin. There's no reason to worry him. No reason to tell him. Not yet.

Yours,
Valerie

CHAPTER FIVE

Renault

"No!" The word is a howl, like an icy wind whipping between the space where the house and the shed don't quite meet. I duck out of the way of the shoe she throws to meet my head, and its hard, flat sole slams against the door behind me.

"Alya. Calm down." If her words are a howl, mine are a snarl, low and fierce, an animal backed into a corner. Because I love my daughter—I *love* her—but tonight, I just cannot take her antics anymore. I need Valerie.

She puts her hands over her ears, wincing as if in pain. "Stop YELLING at me!"

But I'm not. I didn't. I wanted to, but I *didn't*, because as it is, the innkeeper was giving me wary looks at dinner, perhaps sensing the growing storm in her that I, her papa, was somehow oblivious to.

"You cannot scream like that," I say sternly, but it provokes her all the more. Like a child possessed, she tears into my leather satchel, and I catch her around the waist, picking her up, wrenching her fingers off it with my free hand as she wails.

"Sir!" A fist pounds at the door. "Sir, others are trying to sleep!"

That sounds like the other man who'd glared at us, muttering something about chatterboxes who didn't know when to be quiet. How little he comprehended it back then.

"I am aware," I bellow back. "She'll quiet down soon."

"I will not!" Alya kicks my shins. "This is what you get for SCREAMING at me! You're an awful father! You never listen! It would be better if I were dead!"

Never will she speak those words that my heart won't lurch, wounded. With a mighty shove, she wriggles out of my grasp and scurries into the corner, weeping, hands covering her face, wedged into the small space between the bed and the beadboard wall. I shuffle slowly toward the door, unsure if she's even aware of me in her fugue state, but not wanting to anger the man any further. I open the door quietly, but my words are a rush.

"I'm so sorry we kept you awake. My daughter is not well, as you can see."

I expect anger, frustration, pity—anything except the contempt I see in his eyes.

"What kind of man allows his child to speak to him that way? If she were my daughter, I would—"

I hold up a hand, and to my surprise, he stops. "To answer your question, the kind of man who values honesty over artifice. If that is what's in her heart, I would hear it. And in that vein, I do not wish to hear what you would do in my place. Now, I will do my best to keep her quiet for the sake of your rest. Again, my apologies."

"What kind of illness is it?" If I were not a mountain, he could likely see past me, the way he cranes his neck.

I stifle a sigh, his nosiness sucking all the rest of the patience out of me. He's a salesman, I think. Watches. The new kind that use magic instead of simple gears and springs. If I buy one, will he go away? Valerie isn't here to laugh at the joke, and it makes the situation all the worse. She does this for me, talking to strangers, dealing with conflict. I've never appreciated it more.

"Papa? Are you leaving?" She's not hysterical now; Alya sounds almost meek, which can't be right. But maybe being here in this strange place has put her off-balance. Perhaps she does truly think I'd saddle Poppy and ride away without her.

"No, little bird. Now please—nightclothes. You don't have to wash first."

The salesman makes a face, and I grimace. Does he think I don't find it disgusting? I don't want either of us to climb into bed still filthy, reeking of horse. If I'm brave, I'll wait until she's asleep, then sneak down the hall for a bath. But if I'm smart, I'll wake her before dawn so we can slink away, avoiding any lingering resentment from other travelers or worse—advice.

Still disgruntled, the man turns and marches back down the hall. I close the door and pivot to find her turning away from the dresser, her cheeks rosy and scrubbed, having washed a little after all in the basin. I'm practically swaying on my feet; fatigue overwhelms me, and I slump down onto the bed. Alya finds her nightclothes with no help from me, then climbs up next to me, sitting cross-legged on the white sheets. Her nimble fingers stroke the fringe of the blanket. "Papa, will you read me *The Prince's Pony* since I've been so good?"

I've walked in the woods when the hunters have their snares out to catch the bushhoppers, and this feels a bit like that: tricky. Treacherous. "To be honest," I say slowly, "your behavior just now is not what I'd call exemplary. But," I rush on, "I will read you one chapter of our book."

"Two chapters," she haggles, snuggling down into the goose-feather pillow with a yawn, palms pressed together under her cheek. I don't answer, but it doesn't matter; she's asleep before I can read even five pages. It's too easy to blame myself—perhaps we traveled too far. Perhaps I didn't feed her the right foods or give her enough water. I should have taken her to the tavern that would give her fried chicken instead of making her eat the porridge here. But the truth is that even at home, it's a dance, and her moods strike like an adder. I stare down at my girl, then push her mass of golden hair back from her face. My fingers catch, and I realize why people were staring—she has a tangle like a rat's nest near her face, hidden under her hat all day, but revealed at the inn. If I cut it out, her mother will kill me, but I have little to bargain with here. I drag myself from the bed, afraid if I read Valerie's letter there, I'll drop off before I've even washed my face and hands. I stare out the window, the thick evergreen trees across the road waving to me in the wind, as I try to gather my thoughts.

My darling—

Thank you for sending your letter on ahead. I'm pleased to hear more recent news from you. It's strange how even the sight of your handwriting makes my heart beat faster, like I'm catching sight of you across a crowded room, just a glimpse. I want to chase you through a copse of trees and wrestle with you in the meadow. I want to sneak behind the shed and kiss you until the children come looking for us. I want to walk with you under a winter moon, hand in hand.

I'm thankful all is well with you; the Woznick guard and keep you, beloved. We are well, too; Alya tried a new food at supper and she didn't spit it out until she found a table linen. Perhaps just removing her from her environment at home has helped; have we checked the house for spirits or illness hidden between the floorboards? I'm not blaming you, but she's been better this trip, mostly.

And here I pause. Because as a rule, I do not believe in lying to my wife. But also, I don't want her to know that we nearly got ejected from this establishment—she will worry. She'll lie awake at night, fearing for our safety, that neither of us will ever come home. The dangers along the road are very real; I felt the tip of a knife in my ribs just yesterday when a man tried to rob me, but Alya screamed, drawing such attention to him that he ran. To sleep outside would be foolish beyond description, especially with a child. So I will protect my darling wife, my beautiful blade of curved steel, from this knowledge. She's still fragile in a few specific ways from what I can tell.

Our next stop is Sainte-Anne, and then Haguenau at L'Auberge de Mousse Rouge. I hope to see your letters then, too.

Yours,

Renault

CHAPTER SIX

Valerie

"Mama, count my jumps." I'm still trying to finish reading Renault's letter when Clothilde tugs at my sleeve. It's smudged with mud from feeding the chickens this morning, but it hides where the goat kicked me. She's usually so gentle; she must be testy because of the cold. "Mama. My jumps. You count."

Dutifully, I look up from the paper and start the count. "One, two, three—"

"Wait, wait. I need to start over." Tucking the precious letter back into my apron pocket, I take a step into the kitchen—the soup is nearly boiling over. I shift it to the back of the stove, farther from the heat, but I knock into the bread proofing basket with my elbow and it topples before I can catch it. I frown as I brush ash from the dry surface of the loaf.

"Middle of the room, please," I remind Clothilde, who was too sick to go to school, but not too sick to skip rope in the house, apparently. I should bundle her up and send her out into the chilly morning, but it's easier to watch her in here. Ever since Renault's cousin came by, I've been on edge. Sleep has been elusive, even with Renault's trusty crossbow by the bed. I won't need it, I don't think. But I also can't blow out the lamp unless I can touch it.

"Mama," cries Fayette from my bedroom, but the effort sends her into another round of coughing. I hurry toward her, but slip momentarily on the colored pencils someone left on the floor.

"Clothilde, pick those up, please."

"I didn't play with them."

"Not relevant, cherie," I call over my shoulder. Unlike Clothilde, who *definitely* should have gone to school, Fayette is actually sick—her little forehead is burning up when I press my lips to it. *Use your wrist,* I can almost hear Renault grumping, but he's not here, and my lips are better. I think maybe Margot was sick too, but she was too proud to say so and trundled off to school by herself.

"I'm cold, Mama," she whines, sniffling. "It's cold in here."

It's not. I've been stoking the fire all morning to make sure it's not, but I pile another quilt on the bed over the first two, tucking her in tighter. I make her drink a little water before her eyes flutter closed again, her breathing growing shallow as I stroke her curls tenderly. Perhaps I should make her some broth. It would take hours, but it would have more nutrition-al—

CRASH.

"I was in the middle!" The desperate cry comes.

Wincing, I rise from the edge of the bed, not wanting my shouts to rouse my little girl, but I stop short in the hallway when I see what broke. "Oh, you *didn't...*"

Her lower lip quivers as I kneel to retrieve the pieces of my best teapot, the delicate rose and white one I keep on a top shelf...but not high enough to keep it away from stray jump ropes.

"I didn't mean to. I was in the middle."

I never thought I would think this, let alone say it, but when I open my mouth, I say, "I miss Alya." I don't know what brought the thought to the surface, except that I associate her with broken pottery, and that I really miss her.

Clothilde does not seem to know how to take this. She stares at me from above, her big brown eyes doe-like and innocent, then walks over and puts her arms around my neck.

"I do, too." Sisters can be difficult; I don't have any, but I have some very close cousins, so I know it's complicated. These two are always enemies at war or best friends; there's not much in-between. Margot is too level-headed and serious for their silly games and much more interested in mothering Fayette and reading, so Alya and Clothilde are stuck with each other. Except now, Alya is gone. And with all the strife of her wild tantrums, I had not expected to miss her creativity, her beautiful drawings and love notes, the way she could pull us all into a story she was telling.

"What do you miss most of all?" My balance is precarious now, with her hanging on me, but I touch my left hand to the wood floor for support and squeeze her with my right arm.

"Her riddles."

"Oh yes, she tells excellent riddles."

"And the game we play in the barn where we are princesses and everyone does what we want." She giggles. "Even you and Papa."

"No!" I say, faux serious. "Us too?"

"Yes," she says, pulling back to see into my eyes. "Everyone."

"Are you benevolent rulers, at least?"

"Most of the time. But we are very stern with the goats when they nibble our dresses."

That makes me chuckle. "Well, goats need a firm hand, I think. They have no respect for anyone, let alone princesses of such importance." I touch our foreheads together, and she smiles. "From now on, let's skip rope outside, shall we?"

She nods, then swallows hard, like she's about to ask something serious. But she must change her mind, because when she moves away, she goes directly for the dustpan and broom without a word.

As I stand up, I get a strange feeling, and I know that my mother is at the gate. She wouldn't bother waiting for me to open it, but I open the front door and stick my head out just the same.

"Hello, Mother! What a nice surprise."

Her face is still mostly smooth despite her age, except around her eyes and mouth, and they crinkle when she smiles at me. She's wearing the soft purple wrap I made for her last Solstice, dyed with summer frasselberries, and she picks her way carefully down the path. "I saw Margot on her way to school, and she mentioned you could use a hand today."

"I certainly could. Papa doesn't need you?"

"No, he's not in the shop today. His hip is giving him trouble again with this cold."

Clothilde is nearly done sweeping up her mistake when she hears her grandmother's voice. Broom and dustpan forgotten, she runs and leaps into my mother's arms.

My mother grunts, a pained laugh slipping out. "Lala's back is getting too old to catch such a big girl like you," she reprimands gently, but she squeezes her all the same when she sets her down.

"Tea?"

"Yes, thank you. There's frost in my veins from the walk." I nod sympathetically, but I can't bear to linger on the weather as a topic of conversation. That just leads to worry that the snow will come before my loves come back. I would have nothing delay them. I put on the kettle, glancing toward the bedroom. Fayette's still quiet, thank Woz.

"Tildy," my mother says, beckoning my daughter over with a crooked finger, "look what Lala brought you." I recognize my father's work—he's made her a small, covered pan, just right for small hands.

Her eyes are bright. "For shieldnuts?"

My mother smiles and nods. "Why don't you go gather some and we'll make a snack for the four of us?"

Clothilde allows us to bundle her up before she darts out the door, a small wicker basket clenched in her bare fist. I'll be able to see her out the kitchen window. The kettle is singing, so I hurry to pour the tea in a less beloved pot before Fayette wakes.

"Val."

I turn. The last time my mother used that tone, it was to tell me my father had collapsed in the shop from heat exhaustion; he'd needed three stitches in his chin where he met the anvil as he fell.

"What is it?"

She pats the seat next to her. "Come and sit."

I bring the tea with me, but I'm not sure if I want it anymore. "What is it?"

"There's a man in town, asking questions about you and your house. Does your husband really live here? Things like this." She leaned closer. "He even cornered Margot by the apple cart yesterday. She was shaken when I intervened. I nearly sent her home."

From some sleeping place inside, rage surfaces like a whale cresting in the ocean my Margot wants to see. "I'll walk her to school tomorrow. I'm sorry you were put in that position."

My mother shakes her head slowly. "That is not my concern. I was glad to be present to help her. But who is this man? What right does he have to question you?"

"He says he's a cousin of Renault's. He knew him, knew the house. It was his father's, but the family thought him dead. Philippe Cartier."

"There was a Cartier who lived here in Beauchamp, but it was so long ago...I don't know if it was the same family." Her eyes go unfocused as she looks out the window toward Clothilde. "And now he seeks to reclaim it?"

"I believe so."

Her attention comes back to me, observing me the way she does when she inspects my father's work for cracks and fissures. Then she nods once, as if something's been decided.

"Shall I send your father to speak to him?"

"No. I don't think it wise to alert him to Renault's absence, but he may discover it for himself if he's asking questions. He says he's rich now—I don't see why he can't buy another home."

Mother picks up her tea and blows across the surface. "Maybe he wishes to buy it from you."

I watch the steam curl up from my rose-painted cup, just letting it warm my hands, even though I want to throw it to watch it break like the pot that matched it. "He can't afford my price."

"Even if you could use it to pay Madame Montagne? Her help does not come easily."

"Don't know if someone like that has much use for money. Favors matter more," I murmur, unable to sit still, fidgeting in the chair like I'm back in church as a child. She puts a hand on my head, rubbing it a little at my temple.

"I know you've always tried to avoid magical debt, but I believe it will be worth it." She pats my arm soothingly. "I'm proud of you both. You have loved her well. In time, she will appreciate this sacrifice."

I put the teacup down. "If we can even afford it. If Madame Montagne will see them. She may ask a Favor we can't grant. And if we can somehow afford it, the contract is binding forever. You can't sneak out the side door of the church on Seventh Day like you can with the tax collector. Magic always collects."

We let that statement hang in the air, sullying the quiet.

"You're always welcome with us. You know that, don't you?"

I manage a weak smile. "Of course. Thank you, Mother."

"As it happens, it's not just Clothilde whom I brought something for."

I lift an eyebrow, and she just smiles warmly. From the inside pocket of her cloak, she produces a small knife, small enough for my apron pocket. It flips open and closed fluidly when I pick it up, and the handle is carved with butterflies. One might mistake it for a writing plume, if they were unaware...

"It's beautiful. Did I forget my birthday again?"

"This is not for opening wine bottles. This is something more subtle than your favorite pieces to have with you when you go to the gate. Your father made it for Solstice, but I convinced him to let me give it to you early. In case this 'cousin' Philippe comes back." I can't hide my surprise; I've given her the impression that I stopped practicing with the big throwing knives Father and I made when I was a teenager, but apparently, she knows better.

I can hear Clothilde talking to herself as she approaches the front door, and we both get to our feet. Then, impulsively, I give my mother a hug. She seems stunned, because Clothilde has the door open by the time she returns my embrace—I believe the last time I hugged my mother like this was when Fayette was born. It's not that I don't love her; it simply isn't in my nature. Overwhelming, thorough gratitude for who she is and how she understands me compels me to it now.

"I found lots of nuts! Let's stoke the fire, Lala!" Clothilde declares loudly. We shush the girl, but Fayette wakes anyway and I have to lie down with her for a long time before she goes back to sleep. I don't get a chance to write until lunchtime when Mother takes Clothilde to go meet Margot along the road.

My darling Renault,

It's getting cold here. If I had magic to hold back the snow for you, I would certainly use it. If you need to purchase warmer clothes, please don't hesitate. Be careful as you travel. Not much is new here—Fayette has a fever, but my mother is here to help. Clothilde and I spoke of Alya today—the girls have talked little about her since you left, but I think we all miss her. And you, too, of course. Tildy said they play a game where they're princesses in the barn. Maybe I'll ask Father to make them crowns for Solstice; I would see them revel in their power before the world reveals itself as cruel.

I am still hoping against hope that Madame Montagne won't ask a Favor of us when you reach her. Be careful with her, too. If half her reputation proves true, she is not one to trifle with, my love. Be wise. Ask too many questions. Put that wonderful mind of yours to work. Sweet dreams and easy travels.

Yours,

Valerie

CHAPTER SEVEN

Renault

The frost is lingering this morning as we ride north on Poppy. Her gentle footfalls are unhurried, like we're both taking in the sweet scent of fallen leaves and the crispness in the air as we—

"Papa, I need to squat."

I look down at Alya, who's been in a sour mood all morning, despite having a pastry for breakfast.

"We just stopped so you could squat."

"I need to squat *again*."

These sorts of things feel like a younger child to me, more like Fayette, and I wonder for the thousandth time if she'll be like this forever. With a sigh, I pull over along the road at the edge of the woods. It's mostly evergreens on this side, and it should provide her with ample cover for her modesty. Without waiting for my help, she swings her leg in an arc over the horse's neck and slides down his flank, her boots hitting the ground with a thud. My other children would cry, massaging their stinging soles. But Alya turns to me with a smile.

"Be back in a bit."

"Make it quick, please."

"I can't promise that, Papa," she calls, not looking over her shoulder as she disappears into the woods.

Poppy sighs, and I pat her silky neck. "Right." As I look down, I notice the purple-tinged ropeweed climbing on a young fir tree, its tendrils out, and I can't help but smile.

I had asked Valerie to come on a picnic. Her parents were aware of our courtship and approved, based on the nice loaf of bread and bottle of cherry sweetwine they'd contributed to the event. *Event* is not quite accurate—that sounds too formal—but I put effort into the planning, scoping out several spots until I found one sufficiently scenic as well as private enough to let us hold a conversation, but not so private as to be unseemly. It was a long walk, but there was a sandy clearing by the creek a half hour's distance from my home, and I thought it was perfect.

We walked there, hand in hand, each carrying a basket over one arm, and the whole time, my heart was singing. Young love—it does that, even to old hearts. Just to hear her laugh, or see her eyes spark as she told a story...it just delighted me. And she knew so many stories—I don't know if it was being an only child or that rampant curiosity she was born with, but I loved listening to her tell them.

"...and then the old woman transformed into a bird of fire, revealing herself as the witch the boy should've known she was from the start."

I clicked my tongue at her. "You needn't judge him. None of us recognize which moments were the turning point of the story until the end arrives. And that is not how I remember the witch revealing herself."

"So I embellished. Don't you prefer my version?"

"Wholeheartedly," I replied, "but it's still inaccurate." I split off from the main road to cross a small wooden bridge, and Valerie followed me.

"As for my judging him, he deserves it. Who wouldn't realize that an old woman by the road had something up her sleeve? Who just stands there, giving out fruit? It's obvious."

"Perhaps. But I find it relatable, nevertheless."

Valerie chuckled. "You are easily fooled as well."

"A fool, am I?" I dropped my basket and turned to tickle her ribs, but she darted away, laughing.

"I didn't say that, only that you are easily deceived. You see the good in everyone."

"I find that no flaw," I grumbled, turning to retrieve my burden, only to find her right in front of me when I straightened again.

"I didn't say it was." She laid a hand on my cheek, sweeping across it with her thumb, her dark eyes poring into mine earnestly. "Just that you might value having someone by your side who knows a witch when she sees one."

I pressed my hand over hers, relishing the feel of her skin, even on such a warm day, and I turned my head to kiss the inside of her rough palm. She helped her father in the forge often enough to form calluses, and I loved that about her, too.

"How lucky I am," I said slowly, "that you were the one fate sent me, then."

She beamed at me, but as I held her hand and tugged her down the path once more, her expression changed, like the sun going behind a cloud.

"Renault?"

"Hmm?"

"When will you lie with me?"

I halted without warning, and she bumped into me with a small gasp. "You want me to?"

"Of course." Valerie was looking at me like I'd just saddled a horse backward. "Don't *you* want to?"

"Oh, yes. Very much," I said, "but I've been led to believe women aren't as interested in such things."

"You haven't read the books I've read, then."

She knew just how to tease me, even then. How to entice my curiosity and thirst for knowledge, planting facts like a splinter in my mind that only she could remove.

"What books are those?" I asked, a little breathless despite standing still.

Valerie smiled, then with a swish of her skirts, she continued down the path, leaving me with my mouth open and my imagination churning.

"I beg your pardon, but what books are those?" I called, hurrying to catch up with her, only to hear her answering laugh from around the corner. "Answer my question, and I'll answer yours."

She stopped then, but she pulled me off the trail behind a tree wrapped in purple ropeweed, so much that I didn't understand how it could still be alive. When she nodded toward my basket, I placed it on the ground next to hers to take both her hands. And when she leaned forward and whispered what she'd read in my ear, I was very glad both my hands were occupied, so I didn't gather her in my arms right then and there.

"As soon as we're married," I whispered back. "As soon as we make our vows."

"Then let's do it soon," she replied. I breathed in her scent—there was always a little smoke mixed into her herbal soap from passing through the forge, reminding me of the metal in her veins.

"And when our souls are bound together..."

"Yes?" she asked, one eyebrow cocked.

"I would like to try that second thing." Every bird within a half-mile radius took flight at her laughter, and I led her down to our sandy beach picnic with a grin on my face and peace in my heart.

But I've spent too long remembering.

"Alya?" I call. This forest appears as peaceful as that one was, birds still chirping, squirrels chattering. It's when they stop that I worry. "Alya?"

She won't like it if I disturb her privacy. It's the thing she's most touchy about. Anyone who dares approach the outhouse when she's in it should be prepared for an earful.

"Come on, little bird. Let's ride on."

Only a distant creek responds, burbling its soothing song. With a sigh, I dismount, tossing Poppy's reins over a branch on a fallen log. "Alya? Are you well?" Any response would be a relief at this point—her silence is concerning me. "Alya? Answer me, please."

"I'm here." Her voice is small, timid. "But I think...I think I..."

I hope that pastry tasted as good on the way up as it did on the way down, poor thing. When I reach her, she's kneeling next to a patch of victory mushrooms, their fingers pointing to the sky. But a few are broken off, and the scent of them masks her sickness.

"All right, little bird. Let it out." I hold back her hair as she heaves. "We'll stop for the day at the next opportunity."

As soon as her stomach stops ejecting its contents, I scoop her up in my arms and carry her back to where Poppy waits, no longer alone. An old woman wearing a heavy black shawl around her bent shoulders is petting the horse's neck, her gray hair uncovered despite the overcast day.

"Someone was trying to unhook her," she says, offering me back the reins. "You shouldn't leave her alone like that." From where I stand, it looks like perhaps *she* was trying to unhook her, but I push the thought aside.

"A thousand thanks, sister."

She cocks her head at me as I struggle to get Alya up onto the saddle. "Is your little one unwell?"

"I'm afraid so." I stay on the ground, tense, wanting to keep myself between her and my girl, but she comes closer, sniffing the air.

"Smells like mushroom sickness."

"Oh, no," I say, "she simply knelt near them and…" But one glance at Alya's miserable face confirms it. "You did eat them?"

"They're so delicious, Papa," she says matter-of-factly. "And I recognize them. Mama and I pick them at home."

"You must come from down south," the woman says with a knowing nod. "They're safe to pick there. Not here. Too many frimblebugs in the soil, nesting in their tops." The thought makes me want to vomit, but I swallow it down.

"Is there a doctor nearby?"

"All she needs is some wedding flower tea and a few hours' rest. It's a pleasant enough antidote. Please come to my house. I'd be glad to help." My mind hums, hesitating, its gears grinding. Valerie would be certain of what to do. I can never tell the difference between the heroes and the villains, not in real life. But given how green Alya's skin is becoming, I'm not sure I have a choice.

"Thank you, sister. That's kind of you. Please lead the way."

Seeing as she's a widow, I chop a quarter of a cord of firewood for her while my girl sleeps in repayment. No sense in owing more Favors than necessary, and I'll have to pass this way again on our way home, hopefully in less than a week's time. But when the clouds start to sprinkle snow, I make my way inside to sit next to the fire and update my wife.

My darling,

Next summer, let's send the children to your cousin Feline's and go back to our sandy beach, the one where we passed so many pleasant hours before our souls were bound together. I want to lie in its dappled shade with you, holding you, whispering like we used to. Telling each other every secret, listening to your inflated fairy tales with endings so much better than the original tale could spin while flipwing birds dart around us. I want to hear them all.

Alya ate a poisonous mushroom today—she thought it was safe, because we have them at home. Do you actually collect victory mushrooms with her? I couldn't remember if that was the type you use for rice bake with goat's cheese. She is all right now, if that wasn't obvious. A kind older woman stopped to help us, running off someone who tried to steal Poppy as well. Don't worry, I didn't eat any of her shiny red apples.

I hope Fayette is fully recovered, and if not, don't hesitate to send for the doctor. He gets his eggs on credit for just such an occasion.

All my love and devotion,

Renault

CHAPTER EIGHT

I have not had a letter from Renault in three days. The first day, I did not worry. I used the time to finish sheepweaving a soft, cream sweater that Margot has been asking for, working in a wavy pattern that reminds me of the ocean as a sort of promise that when all this is over, I will take her there. She ran her fingers over the bumps, her eyes shining, then flew into my arms, nearly knocking us into the mantel. She's fortunate her mama is the sturdy type.

The second day, Margot put the sweater on to wear to school, and I told her I thought it was too warm...until I opened the front door. The wash of frosty air that met me proved my concern baseless. Once they were gone and Fayette was napping, I took a candle into the attic. Their hats and gloves were boxed up there, I knew, but Renault would usually be the one to climb the steep steps like a crag goat. I lifted the wooden lid, sure to find spiders, but I was instead met with a small green hat with sheepsweave mushrooms all around the edge. I don't cry—there's no help in it—but I felt my allergies to the dusty room acutely as I picked up the small earflap hat.

"Don't you want something cute, cherie? Rabbits, perhaps? Or even toads?"

"Mama," she scolded. "You know I love mushrooms more than rabbits, toads, or even chickens."

She'd managed so much disdain, I'd been almost proud. "Quirky," my mother said when she saw it, and my father just smirked. But I heard she got some compliments on it at school, so I was content with that. I decided to make her another, perhaps in blue, in case this one has grown too small. It will be a pleasant surprise when they come back. If they come back.

Why is there no letter? Is it the writer or the carrier that I ought to worry about? Are they lost, turned about in a dark wood, far from the friendly road, its soft autumn glow lighting the way? Were they attacked? Injured?

I searched through my yarn basket, but I didn't have enough blue even for such a small project. Guylaine will have some; she hadn't sold all of hers yet from their summer shearing the last time I stopped by to chat with her. I resolved to go and get some soon.

On the third day, I clean out the chimney—the smoke isn't rising properly—and we'll keep a fire going constantly as the weather turns toward winter. It's narrow inside, the ridges of the stacked bricks providing tiny footholds better suited for a child, but I don't want them breathing in the dust—the one medical book I have says it's unwise.

But more importantly, there is no room for unwanted thoughts in here while I'm knocking down summer's nests and scraping at the soot. It's too unpleasant to do anything but complain inside my head about the task and the cleanup that comes after, and that is what I need. It's more than believing that they're fine—I feel it in my gut, but my mind sometimes gets in the way. It's more than experience. I can't explain it. It happened when I became a mother—the feeling got stronger, even as indecision and doubt gained footholds like the ones inside the chimney. Intuition, my mother calls it. I'm still learning to listen, even when I make the wrong choices for my family...clearly it's done Alya no favors. I can't help but feel it's all my fault.

I write and send another letter, more out of habit than necessity.

Darling Renault,

I would like to make you aware that I climbed into the chimney to clean it. It was a filthy task, and I know you would have chuckled at the soot on the end of my nose. So if the house burns down, it will be no fault of mine; I would like that noted.

Has she really been so much better behaved along the road? I don't know why that makes me feel so awful. I've long harbored a terrible fear that I make her worse somehow, that we rub each other wrong like sandpaper, being too alike. Perhaps this trip has proven the theory valid.

I cherish your letters, love. I think at this point, you could catalog the flora and fauna in the ditch along the road and I would treasure it still, just to see your hand-

writing, just to have a piece of you. You should see me sniffing your letters just for a whiff of you. Your scent has long faded from the pillow.

We are safe and well; do not worry about us.

With all the love in my heart,

Val

It's unnecessary to hurry into town—the post won't leave for several hours, but the girls will be done at school soon. They kindly dropped Fayette with Feline to give me the time to focus only on my odious task, but she'll wake soon from her nap and be ready for time with me again. My hair is still damp from when I washed, and it's chilling me to the bone, sitting in the wet braid I wrapped around my head. But since I hurried, before I send my letter I have time to buy the blue yarn I wanted, brighter than a summer sky, and I'm perusing the cabbage and broccoli in Celeste's stall, thinking the girls will be along in a half hour's time, when a shadow falls over them.

"Your husband is not home, madame." Philippe. He's standing close to me, in order to hiss into my ear, lest anyone hear his attempt at intimidation, and I can smell the onions on his breath, the sour sweat in the collar of his velvet cape. Being rich doesn't impart taste, clearly.

"Cousin, he is merely ill—"

"So ill, and yet the doctor only comes for eggs..."

He's been watching the house. *My* house. A shiver runs down my spine, but I start forward again into the street, hoping he won't follow. His heavy footsteps dash my hopes.

"Did he leave you?" he asks casually, lengthening his steps to catch up as he shines a red apple on his shirt. "Run off with a woman not so steeped in guile?"

"You were a stranger to me, with no one to corroborate your story. What was I supposed to do, invite you in for tea?" I shift my basket to the other arm, putting some space between us and freeing my left hand at the same time. I'll need it if this comes to blows. I don't think he's that foolish, not here in the village—but then he waves to the baker's wife, and she cheerfully waves back as she rearranges the buns. He's been making friends or perhaps renewing old acquaintances. I've never been good at that...which reminds me what I am good at. I turn into an alley, and he dogs my steps, never seeming to consider where I might lead him.

And not just any alley—the alley behind my father's shop. Our footfalls and breathing sound louder here, bouncing off the bricks. Philippe grasps my elbow, pinching the skin there.

"That house is mine, Valerie. I don't care where you and your abandoned brood go. I don't care if you live in the woods like animals. You will leave my property before—"

He barely even reacts when I turn on him, sending my basket flying. Over the sound of my father pounding on a piece of metal in the forge, no one will hear him cry out—if he could get a breath. Not so easy with his back against the soot-smeared wall, my forearm against his neck, and my new knife against his pulse.

"It is *my* property. And no, Renault did not *leave* me—he took our ill daughter to a healer up the mountain, Madame Montagne. He *will* be back. And at that time, you can discuss your concerns with him." He shifts uncomfortably, scowling.

"And the next time you put your hands on me without permission, be sure you're ready to answer to him *and* me for the indignity." I shove away from him, keeping my knife lifted.

"Mama?" Margot stands at the end of the alley, holding a sister by each hand.

"Hello, girls—they let you out early? What an unexpected pleasure!" I don't bother to look back at Philippe—it would only deepen the scowl between my daughter's eyebrows. I hastily gather up the things that rolled from my basket, trying in vain to brush the dirt from them. "Let's go home, and then we'll make iron cookies—the snap and spice of them is just the thing on such a chilly day." Margot is still looking over her shoulder as I lead them away, but the other two chatter about their day, as oblivious as I want them to be.

Margot is quiet the rest of the afternoon. I steal glances at her, wondering how much she saw and heard of the interaction. I'm sure she would like a mother like the other girls in school—one with an angelic voice in the church choir or a skill for baking delicate cakes or arranging flowers, careful to keep themselves clean and proper.

It takes a little extra time to put the little ones to sleep; the bee's gold of the cookies makes them active, but their small bodies calm and slumber, eventually. I'm sure Margot is asleep when I take my forgotten letter out of my pocket.

"Mama?"

Her dark head appears over the side of her high stacker bed, propped up on one elbow.

"Yes, cherie?"

"Will you always put pockets in my dress?"

Mmm. My girl saw it all, then. I cross to the bed, brushing the hair back from her cheek.

"Yes, cherie. Always."

She gives me a small smile, then turns over. And it doesn't seem to bother her when I break the seal to amend my letter.

Something happened today, something I ought to have told you about before, but I had no wish to worry you. I hope you can advise me or perhaps send a letter to your relatives and let me know of the reply. A man came here who claimed to be a cousin of yours, Phillippe...

CHAPTER NINE

Alya

My stomach feels strange when I awake. I remember where I am—the old woman who led our horse away. It's her house. The whispers told me she planned to keep Poppy, but she sensed an opportunity in Papa; they didn't say what it was. I rub a hand over my sore belly, but I don't make any sound. I'm not ready for my consequence yet for eating the mushrooms that sang to me, that crooked a finger in my mind. The room is mostly dark except for the dying fire, gently playing its light on the ceiling. But when I turn my head to see if they're sleeping, I find that woman bending over his still form, hands hovering over his chest.

"You get away from my papa." My throat feels scratchy when I speak, probably because I threw up so much. Because I was so bad. Shame burns my throat too, forcing unwanted tears from my eyes. The witch spins, her graying hair loose like she's been asleep.

"Oh good, you're awake," she says, her voice like bee's gold, but my whispers stir. They don't like her. I don't either. I don't know why—her outsides are pleasing, her face round, her hands soft. Her home smells like locksbreath and ladylace, flowery and nice. But underneath, there is something else here. Mold. Rust. Decay, like a kitchen waste pile left too long without turning. It is stale and frightening, something to send my sisters howling into the woods. Lucky for Papa, I am not my sisters.

"What are you?" I ask. I want to know for next time. Then no one will take me by surprise.

"Don't you mean 'who are you?'" She smiles, and I see she has all her teeth. Witches aren't supposed to be pretty. "My name is Gitta, remember? You ate my sunbread to settle your stomach after you were so sick." Did I? I can't reach the memory if it's there. Something strange is happening here.

"No, I meant what I said. I know *who* you are. Now I want to know *what* you are."

She tips her head to the side and her eyes narrow a bit. "I do not think your papa would like you talking to me like that."

"Well," I admit, propping myself up on one elbow, "that is true. But my mama would not mind."

"Tell me about your mama, dear girl. Is she powerful with magic?" She reaches toward my hair, but I knock her hand away.

"*Don't* touch me." The whispers get louder, and Gitta looks surprised.

"Alya?" Papa's murmur is half-asleep still, and my whispers tell me he still has one foot in the land of dreaming. I hear him talk to Mama there at night. It's not really her, just memories. But it seems to me that love is a kind of power, like my whispers. Those dreams make Papa stronger, just like her letters. I will make sure he gets back to her.

"It's all right, Papa. Go back to sleep." Just like my sisters, he rolls over, mumbling, and a moment later, his breathing is even again. Gitta is staring at me now, her face a bit gray. "Are you a witch, then?"

"Why, what a thing to say!" she says with a light chuckle, and I notice she's avoiding the question. "How is your stomach, dear? Would you like something to drink?"

I eye the smooth ocean-green teapot. It didn't taste bad, but something tells me no. Something inside knows it's not good. Not for me. Usually my knowing comes from the whispers, from the things I hear, not from scents. But maybe things just work different here.

"Do not all regions have witches? Our village does. It's nothing to be ashamed of."

Her tone is cold for the first time. "Go back to sleep, Alya." Gitta tries to soften the command. "Have happy dreams."

"No, thank you. How long have we been here?"

"You're still recovering, dear. Don't worry about it."

"Where is my horse?" It suddenly feels very important that I find out.

"In the barn, of course. Where else would she be?" She's losing patience, this witch.

I shrug. "Perhaps you sold her to a passing merchant or set her free. She could be many places by now, in that case." Poppy is an old horse, but I love her. The whispers and I are keeping her going on this long journey to see someone who can help our family. At least, that's where I think we're going. We feel...troubled about it. I cannot let Papa get himself in trouble again. If he offers her a Favor, what would that mean for me? For Mama? While I've been thinking, this witch is getting closer, and I startle when I notice.

"Stay back." My voice is firm, but I cock my head, trying to hear my whispers. There are other whispers here, though, ones that tell me this woman is nothing to fear, that I am safe and whole here with her. That I should sleep, dream, rest. I cover my ears, but it does no good—I can hear them still. They're a worse poison than the mushrooms, a more piercing pain. "*Stop that.*"

Papa rouses again, blinking and rubbing his eyes in the low light. "Alya? Are you well?" At the sound of his voice, the other whispers quiet, and Gitta seems more annoyed than ever.

"Well enough. Let's leave." I throw off the quilt, and it suddenly occurs to me that she has a lot of beds for someone who lives alone. It sends a creeping feeling over my skin. It's too late in the season for rustchests to announce the dawn, but I can tell it's nearly morning.

"Leave?" Papa still seems befuddled, and it angers me to think that she did something to him. She was watching the way he worked around the property, cutting firewood for her, repairing a broken window, fixing the wobble in her kitchen stool. He was too useful, I think, for her to let go. I take him by both hands and attempt to pull him from the bed, but he's too heavy to budge. "Why would we leave?"

"I'm better, and this place is no good."

"Alya," he sighs, then casts a look of regret at our host. "I apologize, sister. My girl has a mind of her own."

"You need your rest," Gitta protests, pushing Papa's shoulders back down toward the mattress. The moment she touches him, my whispers become frantic, panicked, like the hens when Papa goes out to their house with the axe. They feel death approaching with heavy footsteps.

"*No.*" My voice sounds strange, like when I shout into a hollow log. I shove her away at her hips, and she stumbles toward the hearth, catching herself against the stones with a hiss.

When she turns, there is no more kindness in her face—it's twisted with a threat she's not saying out loud.

"I know what you are, magic eater. Unnatural scourge! Child of darkness!"

"They were *mushrooms*, witch. Time to go, Papa." I tug on his hands again, and this time, he scoots forward, his feet coming to the floor. Gitta continues to yell, but shrinks back toward the fireplace when I glare at her. I'm too busy tucking Papa's laces into his shoes, helping him into his worn cloak. Our bags are still by the door. She's gone through them, I can tell. Mama's letters aren't in the right order.

I drag him to the barn and thankfully, she was telling the truth about Poppy. Papa's blinking a lot, but he seems to come to himself the farther we get from the house. There's no need to pull him now; he takes the heavy bags from me and puts them on the horse. Gitta follows us with more cajoling.

"Come and have breakfast. I'm sorry I lost my temper. You can't continue your journey on an empty stomach. Please, come back inside..."

Papa turns slowly. "You said some terrible things about my little girl back there. I'd rather ride ten days on nothing than make her sit at your table again. If she wants to leave, we're leaving."

I've got those big feelings Mama talks about right now. They're pushing tears against the backs of my eyes again. I know Papa wishes I was like Fayette or Margot or Clothilde, and I go to sleep every night wishing I could be. But his words wrap me up in a good feeling, and it helps drive away the bad ones in that house. I don't think he's fit for this task, though—he should be tending his chickens and chopping our wood and making Mama laugh. If he stood so poorly against this normal witch, what will happen when we reach this powerful stranger we're going to see?

When we round the bend and put her house from view, Papa leans down to me. "Thank you, little bird. I don't know what happened exactly, but thank you."

I give his arm a squeeze when words won't come.

It's going to be so hard to say goodbye.

CHAPTER TEN

Renault

I think we've lost some time. We were with the woman a while, but I'm not sure how long exactly. Even her name is escaping me, and Alya refuses to speak of her. But when I finally have the opportunity to give my letter to a carrier, he shakes his head.

"They've had a paperfall. Might take longer than expected."

"Already?" I don't relish the idea of returning to Beauchamp with Alya in the snow.

He nods. "Strange, isn't it? Usually, we get it first. Can't explain it. And they're expecting blanketfall by the end of the week."

"Very strange," I agree, but I can't help but be thankful we haven't yet. We've made good time today; the trees are thinning out as we climb. The soil is rockier here, the moss more yellow than the emerald of my little town, stringy and limp as it hangs off the north side of the trees. Not as much bird song either. I can't say it appeals to me. Alya seems eager to travel far today. I know it's serious when she agrees to eat stale bread while Poppy carries us through the lunch hour.

"What frightened you so in that place, little bird? Won't you tell Papa?"

"Nothing *frightened* me. I'm not afraid of anything."

"You'll forgive my bluntness, but it seemed so. You shoved me out the door before my laces were tied."

She huffs impatiently. "That wasn't fear, Papa. We just needed to leave. Do you see the difference?"

"Afraid not, daughter."

"Of course not," she mutters under her breath, but I hear her, and I'm glad my beard can hide my smile.

"Are you worried about meeting Madame Montagne?" I ask.

"Why would I be? It's not me she wants to speak to."

Dread strikes me then like a goat trying to knock the legs out from under you from behind, angling for the food in your hand.

"Alya. I think you've misunderstood."

The look she shoots me over her small shoulder is skeptical and disdainful all at once. "Misunderstood how?"

"Your mother and I want you to meet with the woman to see if...if she can help you."

"Like a tutor?" She does well in school, thankfully. She seems to bottle it all up inside, shaking the feelings like sodawater until she gets home and it all spills out.

"No," I drag out the word, stalling, "not like a tutor. We are worried for you. Your rages. They don't happen to the other girls."

I'm lucky that we did not stop. I can see the anger rising in her. Were she free to leave, I believe she would stomp toward the deerpath leading into the forest.

"Try to understand, little bird. We love you so much. We just want to help. We want you to feel...whole."

"None of you understand me." The words are hopeless, hollow and desperately soft. "You're not really my family."

Tears prick at the corners of my eyes. Even after all this time, it hurts me to hear her say it. I wonder if it will ever stop stinging, or if it will go on and on like when the sun turns my face red, tender to the touch. But my anger rises before I can find out.

"Would a father who's no father at all risk coming all this way if not for love? Would he leave his wife and travel through dark and danger? Would he spend half his meager fortune at inns? I think not."

"You *don't* love me!" she shouts, thumping her hands on the saddle. Poppy bolts forward, jerking us both backward, and instinctively, I tighten my grip around Alya's middle and grip the horse's body with my legs.

"Whoa! Poppy, whoa, girl!" I lean to grab the reins Alya dropped, and then I see what's really spooked her: cavedogs. There's three on my dominant side, the gray fur on their necks prickling as they bare their teeth, and when I turn my head, I can see two more creeping out of the wood.

"Alya," I say, trying to keep my voice even. "Grab the reins. Poppy's afraid of the dogs. Help her be brave like you." I mean, of course, for her to lean down and grab the reins and pass them to *me,* but as usual, this child and I are not looking at the same sky. Setting her jaw, she leans down, breaking my hold on her middle, nearly toppling off the side if not for my grabbing her hood. When she comes up, she jerks Poppy's head back. Her dancing steps slow, and Alya gathers the reins tighter, removing the slack.

"Go, silly horse. Cavedogs can't take us down. No one can."

There's no way Poppy understood her—I know that—but she sets her head forward and trots past the vicious creatures as if they weren't there. They seem as baffled as I am, glancing at each other with cocked heads, but they simply watch as we pass through the group. Once we reach the corner, they turn their attention to a wild rufflewalker. A shudder runs through me as they give chase—they were obviously hungry, and the black and white feathers are now flying. Why did they just...stop?

"Papa."

"Mmm?"

"Are you all right?"

"Yes, I'm well. Are you?"

"Of course," she says, flicking the reins to urge Poppy faster. "Why wouldn't I be?"

Shaking my head, I give her a squeeze. What must it be like to be so divorced from reality? What kind of place does the world seem to her, I wonder. If it only gave her the confidence to prance past threats unharmed, I would praise it. But to misunderstand the actions of others so thoroughly in the face of such overwhelming evidence to the contrary? I don't understand it. What I wouldn't give for an hour in my child's head. To truly understand her heart. We have to fix this. We must.

"Pass Papa the reins, please."

"You seem tired," she says, placidly denying my request. "I'll guide Poppy."

"No, thank you," I say, reaching past her to take them back, and she folds her arms crossly.

"You never let me do anything! You're the worst father in the world." She spits the words more than speaking them, and I'm too exhausted to argue.

"Probably so, lamb. Probably so."

When we finally reach Le Sommet Solitaire—more of a bar with rooms than an inn—there's a letter waiting for me from Valerie, and I can't even wait for the room key to tear it open.

> *My darling,*
>
> *I'm sending this on, hoping it hasn't missed you. We've had a scattering of snow here, and I hope it doesn't mean it has caught you worse. Your cousin is keeping his distance for now, but I believe he's just gathering favor before he tries again. Please, hurry back. We miss you both desperately. And please write back to let me know you're all right—six days really is too long without a letter, my love. I can't imagine what's kept you from writing without my heart beating out of my chest, so I try to keep my mind from it. But I cannot.*
>
> *Give Alya a kiss on the head for me.*
>
> *All my love (and a lot of worry),*
>
> *Valerie*

"Mama sends her love, little bird," I say, skimming it again. *What cousin does she speak of? Six days? I thought only three...*I lift my head to ask the man if there are more letters and suddenly realize something.

"Alya?"

She's not next to me. She must have gone to feed Poppy. I wind through the rowdy groups at scarred wooden tables to push open the front door. The brisk night air greets me, but no Alya. Poppy's munching from a bucket of oats held by the groom, the lantern light unable to make the granite slab walls seem friendly.

"Have you seen a girl? About to my chest, with light hair?"

He shrugs and shakes his head, petting Poppy's neck. My stomach lurches, wrenching around in my belly, despite how little I've eaten today. I turn and search the beer-scented room with my gaze—no little blonde head. She's got to be here. She has to. Surely she's just entertaining the patrons with stories of her antics, making them laugh. I swallow hard. The men here are more of the trader-hunter variety, not farmers like me. Would they take advantage if I share my problem? Is it safe to shout her name, safe to go room to room, pounding on doors until I find her?

Part of me knows, though, that I won't find her. It's a sickening knowing, so strong it's hurting my head, pounding with it. *She's gone, gone, gone.* All the times she threatened to run away, I never believed her. She fears the dark—I know she does. But I gave her something worse to fear—Madame Montagne.

"Sir? Your key." With a shaking hand, I reach out and take it from the junior clerk, thanking him weakly. It's pointless, though.

It's going to be a long night of looking.

CHAPTER ELEVEN

Alya

These woods are a strange kind of dark. They're not like the woods of home, friendly even as the day ends, birds singing each other to sleep. No one says a word in these woods. I've only been walking a short time, but I couldn't tell you which way the inn is. Not that I want to go back—I don't. I don't need whatever the witch offers, and if that's what Papa thought was going to happen, he is very wrong.

But the strangest thing about these woods is my whispers. Some of their voices are...different. I didn't know the whispers had voices, but I can hear them, same as I know a fleet-chested berrybrooder from a horn-puffed snicklesap. For one thing, one new voice is a woman's. Not like my mother or my grandmother or any of my big girl cousins. This voice is smooth like a river pebble. And it uses far more words.

I duck under a low-hanging evergreen branch.

Up so late, little one?

I look around, but in the crinkled black, I can't see very much.

"I suppose so," I whisper back. "What of it?"

The voice laughs a little. My whispers never did that. When they do use words, it's usually just a few: *Mushroom. Flower. Sister.* They don't know how to ask questions.

These are my woods. You didn't ask permission to cross them.

"I didn't know I needed to. I'm sorry." Papa would like those polite words, I think, even though he'd be angry that I ran away. I will try to remember all the things he taught me as I make my new life here in the woods like a proper witch. A better one than Gitta.

Come to my house, and all will be forgiven.

It smells funny here, too. Not all good and brown like leaves dancing to the ground, but like a crust of bread that fell off in the oven, charred and black. I rub my nose.

"I don't know the way." Could I sleep there? It would be warmer than these woods, watching the heavens for snow. All these trees have their eyes up, waiting to see whose branches will catch the first flake. It's a little warmer under this bush. I still have my heavy cloak on, the one Mama made for me.

Why have you left your father, little bird? Maybe I am still sick from those mushrooms, but my tummy clenches, hearing that name. I'm sure many people call their daughters that. I can't think of any in Beauchamp, but Papa is an Elsewherer. Perhaps he learned it where he's from. When I don't answer, my whispers get nervous, but I shush them.

Who's that with you?

"No one." That's what I've learned to say. *No one.* Otherwise the grown ones think you're silly or empty-headed.

They speak to me, too, you know. They're broadcasting my voice to you now.

I don't know what broadcasting is, but I imagine it's like casting a line into the lake, hoping for a wide-mouthed prisset to bite.

"How? Will you teach me?"

It would take a long time. Do you think you'll be with me that long?

"Alya!" That's Papa. He sounds more scared than the time he thought Fayette fell into the lake. He sounds terribly worried.

"Where are you, little bird? Please, come out. Let's go back to the inn and get warm. I'm sorry if I frightened you. You don't have to go see her. Let's just go home, first thing in the morning. Please."

Do you want to go home with him?

"He doesn't understand me." The wind carries my whisper, and he turns his head.

"Alya? Please, let's work out a plan together. I want to listen."

Is he unkind to you?

I shake my head, but dare not make a sound. I don't know if she can see me, but I hear her hum, a thinking sound like Margot doing arithmetic.

Would you miss him if you came to live with me?

To live with her? I'm striking out on my own. No one's going to take that away from me.

Mm. You need freedom. I see that. But I wonder what you might learn from this person he's taking you to see? Could she help you live in harmony with those you love?

When I don't answer, she goes on.

You can always have your adventure later, can't you?

It's true. I love Mama and Papa, but between the chickens and us girls, they're very distracted. I could run away again, if I wanted. And it might not be winter then. I'm already hungry.

But I still don't stand up. It's too hard. Then I hear Papa crying. I peek out from my bush, just a little. He's sitting on a fallen log, head in his hands, his shoulders shaking. Snow is collecting on them, and I suddenly feel sorry for making him sad. I knew he would be angry, but I didn't think he'd cry. The witch's words echo in my mind—he asks for too much, things I can't give him, but my family does love me. And I love them. I should give him another chance.

I'm quiet, so Papa doesn't hear me coming, but when I wrap my arms around his neck and lay my head on his shoulder, he just cries harder. Big, heaving sobs pour out of him, wetting his beard.

"It's okay, Papa," I whisper, and my whispers purr their approval. They've always liked Papa. "It'll be okay." He turns to bundle me up in his arms then, squeezing me tight in that way I like, as if he's a treesnapper snake.

"I'm sorry. I'm so sorry I frightened you. I'm trying, little bird. I promise I am."

"You're doing a good job, Papa," I say, trying to console him. I really want him to stop crying. It's making me squirmy, and he loosens his hold. I stroke his wet head a little. "Where's your hat?"

"Oh, I...uh, I lost it." He wipes his runny nose on the back of his mitten, and I step back, because...ew. I pat his shoulder.

"Is there still dinner? I'm awful hungry."

His tears have slowed now, and his mouth hooks into half a smile. "Awful hungry? Not well-behaved hungry? Not terrible hungry?"

"Papa..." I say, rolling my eyes. "How can you joke at a time like this?" I hope there's chicken. I really love chicken. Unless it's one of ours. He gets to his feet, but presses me to his side right away, like he's afraid to lose me in the dark. He doesn't need to worry.

I'll see you tomorrow, little witch. Sleep well.

Tomorrow? I'm going home tomorrow. Papa said. Maybe I imagined those whispers, but I don't think so. Her words make my stomach feel strange, like I carried the strangeness of the woods back with me, swallowed like too many bubbles in doubledown tea, the kind Harriet sells in glass bottles with the stoppers. My sisters like skymelon, but it's tooptoop root for me—spicy, sweet, extra bubbles.

No, she's wrong. I'm not going to see her. I'm going home.

CHAPTER TWELVE

Madame Montagne

The magic is crimson with grief today. It floats in front of me, wispy and despondent, a blobby mess. All these weeks, it has been waiting to get to know this girl. She outsmarted the witch who tried to steal their horse. She stared down the cavedogs. She even refused my invitation last night, despite all the pinks and purples, all the sweetness I poured into it. I had thought that once they arrived, parting her from her father would be easily done. Now I see that won't be the case.

Despite the magic's melancholy, when I push back the sheets, it lights the fire for me, a rainbow of color sparking around the cold logs before settling back into a more average orange. But there's no time to tarry if I'm going to catch them. I'm quiet as I gather my cloak and gloves, pocketing the meagerest breakfast of ironsnaps and a small lilletfruit, its citrusy peel fragrant against the winter chill. But he still hears me. My father appears in the doorway, still in his nightgown and striped cap, looking more like an old man than usual.

"Mireille? Are you trying to beat the sun to his route?"

I smile. "No, Papa. Just a bit of business to see to this morning. I'm meeting my new apprentice."

His bushy white eyebrows hunker together as if for warmth on his brow. "Apprentice? You can barely stand your nephews. What would you do with an apprentice besides resent him?"

"Her," I correct, pairing it with a kiss to his scratchy cheek. "I'll see you at the midday meal. Please tell Liesel."

"Very well, but who's going to make my oatmeal?"

"Liesel will, Papa. She knows how you like it."

"With dried pitclumpers?"

"Of course."

If I had to guess, he's as anxious for his routine to be preserved as he is about me leaving the castle. I haven't since the summer Solstice; the world seems content to come to me, and I can't complain.

"And grated swirlbark?"

I sigh on my passage down the hall, calling down the stairs. "Liesel?"

"Yes, my lady?"

"Please see that Lord Frost gets his breakfast, just the way he likes it."

Her voice floats up the stone steps as I descend. "Swirlbark and pitclumpers?"

I turn to give him a smug smile, but he's not behind me.

Where? I ask the magic, and it draws me a moving picture in green of the old man, putting on his robe and slippers to come downstairs. Green? He's jealous? Perhaps I should bring him. I've always thought of him as a homebody, happiest among his books and plants, but perhaps I'm wrong.

"Papa?"

"Yes?"

"Would you like to come with me? You'll have to put on speed."

There's a pause, and I can nearly feel his conflict in the air.

"You can have your porridge when you get back, even if it's midday."

"I'll be ready in a blink, dearest."

Harbor and Shade are already harnessed when I arrive in the stables. The magic must have come out to speak to Nurifa on my behalf. The blind old giantess stoops to reach out a hand to me.

"All ready for you, Enchantress." Giants are such perfect people to handle nightstallions—both feel larger than life, and the giants seem to have a calming influence on such wild beasts. Maybe it's because they can both pass into shadow and unsubstance, or maybe it's just that both are very far from home, and that knowledge speaks to both souls. But either way, she didn't come to me from across the Sparkling Sea for work. She came for refuge.

"A step ahead of me as ever, Nuri. Thank you." I give her finger a squeeze. "We'll be back around midday if all goes well." Papa's not dressed for the cold when he comes outside, but Liesel's not far behind, her pointy ears having picked up our discussion, draping a soft white scarf around his neck, and holding out his leather gloves. Her long strides overtake his shuffling steps easily and she drapes another red plaid blanket around his broad shoulders.

"Oh, quit fussing, girl. It's a morning ride, not a transcontinental journey."

I can still feel Alya, but just barely. They must have started off.

"Speed, Papa. My apprentice has left without us." Between Liesel and Nuri, they get him on Harbor with little issue, and we trot toward the gate, their heavy hooves packing down the dusting of snow on the cobblestones. They are mostly here right now, my nightstallions. The wind is calm right now and isn't stealing their corporeality as it sometimes does. They're not native to these lands; they were forced from their homes. It's to my advantage; they have all the power and none of the aggression and fear their kind learns from the herd, and they were already broken to a saddle and bridle when I received them. More refugees, of a sort.

We pick up speed down the hill as the road winds its way toward the village. Papa tries to rub his hands together, but it does no good through the gloves. In my mind, I draw a picture of warming our hands by the fire for the magic, and immediately, I feel the heat.

"Thank you, Mireille," he says with a smile. "Now, what is it about this girl?"

"I spoke to her the other night in the woods. Her father was bringing her to see me, but he appears to have changed his mind." And at the speed he's going, he's going to work that poor old horse to death. He likely fears the snow; he'd have no way to know I'm coming. Unless...

"Why did he seek your help?"

"The child has outbursts which they find difficult. Her emotions are dysregulated due to interactions with the magic."

My father turns his head to look at me. "We know something of that, don't we?" There's no judgment or upset in his gaze or his tone, and I can't deny the facts.

"Hers are more disruptive to her family life, I believe, but yes. I'd like to help them if I can."

"At a cost?"

"I can't function any other way." The set of his jaw, even hidden behind his sheepsweave scarf, is disapproving. He leaves the statement be, but I argue with myself about it the rest of the way down the mountain.

If I don't ask for Favors, too many people will come, and for foolish reasons. I'm not a wart remover. I don't want to spend time finding lost whiskerfurs or people's spectacles. The point of the Favor is simply to have people consider the cost. I never even collect on most of them.

But if I didn't ask a Favor, maybe more who had nothing to trade or barter would come. Those truly in need like Liesel and Nuri and the others. He didn't turn around because of the cost, but how many never made the journey at all because of it? How many were deterred by the very idea of dealing with someone like me?

We don't catch up with them for nearly two hours, despite the nightstallions' greater speed than their old chestnut. When the pair comes into view, Alya is singing a song about a rabbit who finds a silk hat, braiding her horse's mane like it's a sister, while her father is nearly nodding off behind her. He stayed up most of the night, afraid she'd try to run again. Seeing Shade startles him wide awake, though. He pulls Alya closer and pales when we approach.

"Renault of Beauchamp. I believe you were coming to see me."

He nods jerkily. "I'm sorry, but we've changed our minds. I'm sorry you were put to trouble on our behalf."

"If I was," I say lightly, "it seems it is because I have chosen it myself, so you needn't apologize." I shift my gaze to the girl.

"Hello again, Alya, daughter of Valerie. You didn't come to my house after all."

She's still braiding, even though we've all stopped now, her blonde head bent over it like a jeweler with his magnifying glass.

"Hello, witch."

"Alya," her father groans. "Address the lady with more respect, please."

"Why? Is she rich?"

"Do only rich people merit respect?" I ask.

She quirks her lips to one side, then the other. "Sometimes they don't merit it at all."

"True enough," Renault puts in, "but let's consider her worthy until we learn otherwise."

I pull the soft leather pouch from the hidden pocket inside my cloak. "Renault, I have brought you a potion."

Her head lifts at that, and I hold it out for her father to take. Warily, he eyes it, but does not accept it. "May I inquire as to the nature of this gift?"

"Of course. This liquid will make your daughter like your other girls. More obedient, more malleable."

He stares down at Alya, then lifts a hand to stroke her braided hair. "No. Not that."

"What, then? More docile? Less energetic?"

"No, my lady. I just..." I've put him on the spot in front of his daughter, but I had no choice. He was going to leave with the most powerful magic user I've encountered in years, and that would be to no one's benefit, especially if she's struggling.

His voice drops in volume and in pitch. "I just want her not to hate us so. I want her to know our deep love for her."

Alya looks like she's ignoring him, but she hears. I know she does. I heard, too—all the priests and tutors and nannies and doctors. The fact that I didn't speak until I was six shouldn't have convinced them I was deaf or stupid.

"You know," my father starts, "the magic puts demands on her, too. That's what we found, as Mireille grew. She could tell us more about how it felt, why asking for things that seemed simple to us was so intolerable to her. Why it made her so angry and despondent."

"No, the village witch told us it wasn't magic. She…"

"Was mistaken," I say with a shrug. "There are many kinds of magic, and the one your daughter interacts with is difficult to detect. It's very…intertwined."

"Mireille needed different things than our other children. We had to learn a different way with her. It wasn't an easy road, but having a mentor would have been invaluable."

"I apologize, sir, but who is Mireille? And who are you?" Renault doesn't sound defensive, just tired. I feel his deep long-ing for his wife, and just for a moment, my soul echoes the ache for the one I lost. The magic is drawing…Little speech bubbles appear around Alya, as if illustrated in a children's book, and she cocks her head, then nods.

"No, the apology is mine, good sir. I am Lord Frost, this fine lady's father. We invite you to come to our home for a meal and perhaps to sleep, that we might speak more about this."

Renault scratches his gray temple a little, under the edge of his hat.

"I'm sorry, I don't—"

"It's all right, Papa. I'll go. I won't fuss."

"What?"

"We met in the woods last night. Well, our voices met. I never saw her face until now. She said I could come to her house, but I didn't want to. And then you found me."

Without warning, Renault pulls the reins over to one side, turning the horse to face us. "You approached my daughter? Without my consent?"

"Alya trespassed on my land. Even if she had not, I wasn't aware that holding a conversation with someone without their father present was forbidden. How fortunate that I brought mine with me." To his credit, my father does not laugh. But the magic does. It looks like the fire did this morning, a mess of rainbows and silent mirth. And I know Alya hears it, because she smiles, too. Renault merely looks chagrined.

"I apologize once more, my lady. I'm sorry, this is all very...difficult. Her adventure last night was frightening. I suppose I should be glad you found her and not someone who would wish her harm."

He squeezes the girl again, as if to reassure himself.

"Can we go to her house, Papa? She said she'd show me how to cast my voice like she does."

The woods are still and quiet, but I can hear a wagon coming up the road from the other direction. At the corner, the woman stops short, watching us. Then slowly, she turns the horses back the way she came, her wagon wheels running off the edge of the gravel, tipping a canvas bag out. I ask the magic to return it to her, drawing a picture of the bag floating back into her cart. A few moments later, it does. Renault watches the bag return to the cart as if by an invisible hand, and a ghost of a smile passes over his face.

"Very well, my lady. We are your guests for a time."

"Excellent." When we turn to go back up the mountain, my father and I take up on either side of Renault, and the two men strike up a conversation about the horses. But Alya's focus is on me, her curiosity obvious.

Perhaps it won't be difficult to convince her to stay after all...depending on what I ask for.

CHAPTER THIRTEEN

Valerie

I burned myself again. It's a minor one, unlike last night, when I had to send Margot outside to break some ice off at the edge of the creek. But it wouldn't have happened either time if I could keep my mind on my work. I haven't been able to let my new knife out of my reach since my confrontation with Philippe, and every strange creak of the trees outside has me jumping.

"Mama. Your turn."

Margot is reading between turns as we play chess because I'm taking too long to get back to her, trying to stir the supper I got a late start on and help Clothilde with her sheepsweave when she gets to the end of the row. Fayette is amusing herself somewhere, and that's distracting, too—last time she did, I lost all my good perfume, and my room reeked for days. How has it been only two weeks? They should have arrived at the mountain days ago if nothing delayed them. I know the inns are fewer and the mountain folk keep more to themselves, but I expected...something. More than what we've heard, which is nothing. Nothing. I'm hearing ghosts in the chimney that I just cleaned, imagining Renault's laughter out near the barn. He couldn't be back yet, but I look out the window anyway.

What if he doesn't come back? There's too many of us to stay with my parents for long; could I take over my father's forge if I needed to? I don't have Renault's talent with the animals; they tolerate me at best, whereas they trail after him like he's made of grain. More than once, I had to kiss him gently, holding myself away, because there was a chick in his shirt pocket, keeping warm. Grief and fear are marbled inside me, swirling in sickening ribbons through my soul. I need him back. Not just to run the farm, but because I need him.

I move my queen's side knight to the edge of the board, abandoning the middle of the board. Margot has a clear path to my king with her bishop if she just takes my pawn, and she frowns at me as I turn to reclaim the dropped stitch that's making Clothilde throw her would-be scarf down perilously close to the hearth. The wind shoves against the house, and I feel it whistle through the gaps around the back window, the black, spindly trees dancing beyond the glass, casting shadows against the barn wall from the light of the moon. The soup bubbles over, hissing against the hot iron, and Clothilde asks if Margot can help with the sheepsweave because Mama's taking too long.

"I'm busy," she says, eyes still on her book, and Clothilde bursts into tears about how she never wants to help her. A loud thump sounds in the other room, and Fayette howls at the exact moment someone knocks on the front door. The two bigger girls fall suddenly silent, their gaze on me. *Did I not close the gate? Who would open it and let themselves into the yard unless...*Renault? Fayette is still wailing, and I run to get her first.

"Mama?"

"Don't open it," I say, and Fayette quiets as I pick her up, taking in my hurry with wide eyes. Through the curtain, I can see two figures, maybe three, their washed shadows watery against the red curtains embroidered with white flowers on the front door. I push it back, but I can't see who it is until the one in front lifts a lantern. It's Jacob Pluie, whose wife Selene bought eggs from me just this morning. His jaw is set grimly, and when the lantern swings in the wind, I can see Philippe behind him. And I know why he's here—he manages the town land records.

"Madame Renault," he calls through the small glass panes in the door. "Can we please come inside?"

"You know my husband is not at home," I call back, a sharpness to the words. "How dare you trespass on my property, here in the dark of night? But no. That is your way. Better this way, isn't it?" I'm gaining steam now, emboldened by the locked door. It was like this once before. A different tide was rising then, but just as inevitable. We'd been married only a short while, but I remember it clearly. The acid taste of fear in my mouth as the flood waters rose in the creek. "Yes, better that way, where no one sees. Better not to see that you bully one who may be a widow!" Margot gasps, and it only hardens my resolve.

"Madame, please."

The feeling—that flood feeling—hits harder, overwhelming me, almost begging me to use it, to let it run roughshod over my better judgment. I recall the first time with such ferocious detail—the smell of wet earth as the rain hammered us, Renault shouting to release the animals lest they drown, and the wide, terrified whites of their eyes as I obeyed without argument for once.

But after I obeyed, I went back outside, wading into the muddy water as it crept toward us, lapping at my leather boots, ruining them. I didn't want them ruined—they were my worst pair by far, suitable only for mucking out stalls or crawling under the house, perhaps walking in the marsh—but that's not why I took them off. I took them off because it called to me, the wind.

That's the only way I know how to explain it. It enticed me, tempted me, until I stood in the freezing water, barefoot, staring up at the trees. Renault's voice was nothing, then. The farther I waded into the water, the farther it receded; I couldn't get more than ankle deep. And still the wind hounded me, frigid mud squelching uncomfortably between my toes, my soaked clothes clinging to my skin, heavy as an anchor. The water ran from me.

Renault walked beside me, begging me to think of the baby growing inside me as I shuffled forward, step by step. But eventually he gave up and wrapped me in a wool blanket, his arms around me from behind, lest I fall into the deeper part. We walked those waters back into their banks. We were the only ones in Beauchamp who lost no animals that night.

"Madame, just a word, please. It is late."

"You have a word, monsieur, and it is no. You will not enter this house. Not while I'm the master of it."

"You are a usurper!" Philippe's roar came through the door. "This house is mine by birthright! My father should never have given it away, let alone to that worthless, awkward lump of a cousin!" The crack of a windowpane stuns me for a moment; he must have thrown something, because a row starts outside, three men arguing—Jacob and whoever he was with incensed that he would damage the door and frighten the children, even though my children are still silent, clinging to my waist on either side.

"I am the master of this house," I whisper, blinking hard to release a tear onto my cheek that cannot be wiped away, my hands holding my children too full of them. "I am the master of this house." And that's when it happens. I thought one of them had struck another, causing him to stumble into the door, but despite the spiderglass pane, I could see their shapes receding, moving toward the east end of the property in unison, their arms flailing strangely.

"Madame Renault!" came Jacob's frightened voice. "Please, the wind is unbearable!"

"Then go home!" I bellow at the door. "Go back where you belong and leave us alone!"

The wind batters the door again, and I hear them cry out. With the shadow of their flying hats and cloaks silhouetted in the moonlight, I might have thought they were puppets, put on for the children's amusement. They stumble around for a minute, but the wind is decided: they move toward the open gate, which strangely does not slam shut in the face of it. And when it closes behind them, the air stops whistling through the cracks around the door as well. For just a moment, all is quiet.

Then Fayette claps her hands with glee, and laughing, the other two join her.

"Bravo, Mama!" Margot exclaims. "You've repelled them, with only a word!"

I kiss the top of their heads, too stunned for words. The force of will that kept me going through that interaction is waning now, the energy drained out of me like so much water, whistled away in a forgotten kettle. "Nightclothes," I say wearily. "Let's eat by the fire and read." Perhaps most miraculously of all, none of them complain, unbuttoning their dresses for each other as if it was their idea. The moment they're asleep, I fill the sink and submerge the dishes to keep the pests away and drag myself to bed, too.

This was a temporary solution, and perhaps not the wisest one. If Renault turned around now, he'd still be weeks away. Phillipe will be back, and who knows who he'll bring with him? I slip between the cold sheets, shaking from more than the winter air. Reflexively, I squeeze the knife under my pillow, the crosshatched steel of the handle biting into my fingers.

I need a plan.

CHAPTER FOURTEEN

Renault

The pressure of being on the road for so long is finally ebbing. We spent the day yesterday walking around the grounds, marveling at all the herbs, spices, and other plant life foreign to me, growing bountifully despite the coming snow. We chatted with Mireille's giantess in the stables—I did not know such creatures still existed in the world—and the pointy-eared one whose kind I do not know. But even as we eat her magnificent food, gaze at her fine works of art, let our limbs warm by the high fires and with many cups of tea, I can't help but remember that her wealth is in part sourced by people like me. People who owed her. I want her help—I do. I was wise enough to refuse the potion she offered to "fix" Alya on the road; she admitted it was a test.

"A test?" I say, wrapping both hands around the white mug her maid Liesel offered me with a nod.

"Yes. I wanted to see what kind of man you were. I have watched you both from a distance, as I was able, but there's still a risk for me, getting involved with a family like this. I would make Alya my apprentice, if you agree." Those ice-blue eyes don't miss much, from what I can tell—with her high cheek-bones and long, elegant nose, she reminds me of a queen of old, up here in her castle high above it all, her skin pale from not enough sun.

A risk for her? I look again at the fine tapestry hanging above the mantel—a red winter flower, folded and bent into a spiral, blooming despite the snow. I flex my toes against the soft rug under my feet and inhale the robust scent of the imported coffee I'm about to sip. I cannot offer any treasures such as these. Our entire farm would hardly even match the livestock she already owns; if making Alya her apprentice is half as expensive as I suspect, we'd have to indenture ourselves to pay even half the debt. The house is warm no matter what part I'm in, and I know they have plenty of food. The creatures seem happy here—I'm a good enough judge of that. So I know Alya would be well cared for here too, but as I watch her playing in front of the fire with some paper dolls Mireille pulled out from a closet somewhere, I can't help but have doubts.

She's small, yet. She does not think so, but children don't seem to have much of a sense of scale in that way. Like the blooming flower, she's on her way to becoming a young woman, but she doesn't yet bleed with the full moon like her mother and her sister. She needs them yet, to teach her about strength and courage and beauty and wisdom.

From the latest letter, I'm needed at home as fast as Poppy can fly, and Valerie and Margot have both had ample opportunity to prove these virtues in dealing with my cousin. It's heavy on my mind. I could leave Alya here for the coldest part of the year, make my way back to the others faster, hopefully in time to head off more confrontation. She'd have time to work with the enchantress, and I could return for her when the matter is settled and the pass is clear.

But...this isn't her home. She's happy to pass a few hours here, but without me, would she be comfortable? Content?

"And the cost of this apprenticeship?"

To my relief, Mireille doesn't pretend, but her voice holds a note of regret. "I always ask a Favor."

"Did you have one in mind? Because I'm a man about to live in the trees. I've almost nothing to offer."

She sets down her delicate teacup, frowning. "You have no home?"

"As near as I've ever come, yes. My cousin, once thought dead, seeks to reclaim his father's land and the house thereon."

Her long black hair falls forward as she leans closer to me, shaking her head. "He must be very foolish if he's willing to challenge your wife openly."

This takes me by surprise. "You know my Valerie?"

She rubs her thigh through her wool dress, and the room warms a little like she just stoked the fire. "Just a little. Alya's magic speaks to mine, and she thinks of her mother often. She remembers far more than you can imagine, by the magic's power."

"Speaks?" I ask, hoarsely. "I had no idea the discourse she had with it. And as I told you, the village witch told us it was naught to do with magic." I feel like a fool for believing Jeanette now, but how was I to know?

"Papa, can I play with this?" Alya holds out a stringed wooden instrument that looks to be from my father's father's time, and I suck in a shocked breath, taking it from her gingerly.

"Afraid not, little bird."

"I'd be really careful..." When she sees the unmoved opposition on my face, she turns to Lady Frost, but the enchantress is shaking her head as well.

"Your papa said no."

"But it's *your* house. If you say yes—"

"And why would I do that and make an enemy of your father? I want him to like me, so that we can work together for years to come. I'm building a relationship with him now, and it's only a seedling. But if I am patient and we both offer each other trust, it will grow into a mighty tree. I could cut the sapling down now in order to give you what you want, but it would benefit us both more to show him some support."

It's very grown-up talk for such a young child to my mind, but Alya's gaze is thoughtful as she continues to look at the object of her desire. "Everyone tries to control me. I grow tired of it."

"I know. It will not always be so. Offer them trust, and they will offer it back. I would not wish to see you become the queen of a kingdom of one, able to do whatever you like, but without love and family and alliances. That's an empty life, Alya." When my daughter says nothing, Lady Frost nudges her with her silk-slippered toe. "And I know your papa does not wish to owe me more Favors. I'm curious if you've looked at my books at all. There are fairy tales. New ones."

It makes demands on her, they had said on the road, and I can see it now. Wanting to avoid any further burden, the enchantress asked without asking an actual question—she merely noted the books instead. A diversion; it was Alya's choice to investigate them or not. No coercion, no manipulation. Interesting. We haven't tried this tactic yet, and I see the wisdom of it, if the magic's power is draining her energy for other requests.

"Speaking of the Favor," I say, keeping my voice low, but she motions for silence.

"You say the house is yours? And the land? Your wife has not yet ceded it to him?"

"As far as I know..."

"Then in good conscience, you can fulfill my Favor."

A tug-of-war inside me starts up again, half my heart telling me to run, the other half telling me she understands us, that she's the closest we've come to answers. But more than that, my whole heart agrees that she's kind. It's in the way she deals with her staff, speaks to her father, who's currently dozing in an armchair across the room. If she is truly like Alya, maybe being her apprentice is exactly what she needs, and I'm not. It may cost me everything I own...even my freedom. It would be worth it, and I know Valerie feels the same. This enchantress, as the strange ones call her, she's not wicked. I know she could have forced Alya away from me in the dark, but she allowed her to come back to me. She knew we still needed each other.

"Ask it, lady, and I will tell you."

CHAPTER FIFTEEN

Valerie

Word will spread quickly about that night, and now people are whispering about me, about us, I'm sure. When I look in the mirror in the morning to braid my hair into a crown, I see only Valerie—the strange muscles of my shoulders standing tall, still bigger than most women's from the years I worked in the forge. I see dark hair and tired eyes, the wrinkles of my face somehow deeper these few weeks. But my fear is that no one will look at me that way ever again.

When the magic made the waters recede, Renault asked me how long I'd known I was magically inclined—I said we discovered it together, and he took it as truth, because that's the way we are together. But how many of the people who've known me since birth will accept it? It's been three days since Philippe came, and yet, I've been feeding the children only what I can put together from my pantry because I'm afraid to go out. Afraid to see if he's poisoned them against me.

I walk the children to school again, and as we pass my father's shop, my mother offers to take them the rest of the way. She lets them skip down the snowy lane ahead of her, and I'm thankful they don't feel the same heavy fear hanging around them that I do. I move into the warmth of the forge and take in its familiar scent: metal and woodsmoke and leather. Even the steady noise of the bellows, pumping air into the flames, makes me breathe a little easier.

My father looks up from his work, wiping his hands on his tan leather apron. "You won't let me stay the night? I can sleep by the hearth, in the rocking chair. I won't be any trouble."

I pat his bulky shoulder tenderly. "It's bad for your back, Papa."

"And knowing my daughter and her family might be in danger is bad for my soul. The fear wrests sleep from me, regardless."

"I'm fine. We're fine. I let him know whose land he was trespassing on, and he left."

"Not quite the way I heard it—"

"Perhaps we can discuss this later." In truth, Jacob Pluie's oldest boy just poked his head into the shop, and I don't wish him to overhear our conversation. I notice that I'm not the only one who straightens when he comes deeper.

"Madame Valerie. I hoped I'd find you here when you weren't at home."

"Young Pluie," I reply, not knowing his name. It's an odd way to refer to me; even widows use their spouse's name. "Were you looking for eggs? Or did your mother have you bring washing? If you bring it around later, I can hang it in the barn if you don't mind the scent of—"

"My father has written you a letter." He holds out the paper, folded and sealed with red wax, and Papa takes it because he's closer. "But he said to tell you sorry from my lips as well and ask for your reply." With my children off to school and Fayette in Mother's arms, I really have no excuse to leave. To let my hands shake in private as I break the seal instead of here in the forge. It's only the three of us, but someone could walk in.

Madame Valerie—

I want to apologize for my part in the fiasco of the other night. Had I known Philippe would act so boorishly, I would have insisted that we set up a meeting at some neutral location. I hope you and your children were not frightened.

Your husband's cousin has gone to the magistrate's seat to plead his case. I believe he will be back within the week. I wish there was more I could do for you. Would you allow Baron to sleep in your barn as a safeguard? He could run to get me when that horrid man returns. I have no intention of allowing the law to come between Beauchamp and our favorite egg suppliers. I do not know what the magistrate will say, but at that time, my jurisdiction may be overruled. With Renault's uncle decomposing and his wishes unknown in light of his son's reappearance, they may grant it to him by ancestral right. I urge you to make plans to vacate if necessary—obtain lodging for your animals at the very least, lest they fall into his hands. When I came to your door, I hoped you had papers, a deed, a letter—anything to prove your claim on the house. If you have any such items, be sure you can find them at a moment's notice.

My wife's just come in, and she hopes you'll come to tea soon. Please let us know how we can support you—all of Beauchamp finds this man odious, and I have spread word of his terrible behavior. We are on your side entirely.

Jacob Pluie

Master of Records

There is a difference between coming from a place and belonging to it, I think to myself, as outside, Baron's horse stamps impatiently in the cold. Until now, I was from Beauchamp—it was a starting point for my life's journey, but nothing more than the moving screen behind the puppet show of my life, a painted scene, flat and irrelevant. But since my discussion with Margot about the ocean, I have spent hours trying to imagine my life anywhere else, and though I can't account for why, I have no wish to leave. It's not only for the nearness to my family; I need the tall trees here, the little stream behind the barn, the gentle way the sunlight breaks through my bedroom window. It's only as it's being torn from my grasp that I realize how much I might actually like it here...and how much I've been the outsider because I deemed it so, not because anyone else did.

I belong to Beauchamp, and it belongs to me.

I raise my eyes to the boy in the wool coat and heavy trousers. "You'll be comfortable in my barn?"

"Yes, Madame Valerie. I'll be just fine. I likes animals, and they likes me." I try not to make a face at his grammar, realizing he should also be at school at this moment. He has need of it, apparently.

"Please tell your father I accept his offer. All of his offers."

Baron grins, and something tells me he's going to enjoy being the herald riding through town whenever Phillipe has the misfortune to come back. He's back on his horse and headed down the road when my father speaks.

"You'll take his help, but not mine? That's a fine piece of pie."

"Oh, hush. You can sleep in the chair. But I'm low on salve for the pain, so I'll hear no complaining. Bring your own or suffer in silence."

He kisses my cheek loudly. "Very well, Madame Valerie," he teases as I wind past the anvil and the barrels of stock metal, but the new name suits me. Rather, my own name suits me. If—no, *when*—Renault comes back, I believe I'll keep it. Papa insists on walking me home, and we both turn at the sound of heavy hoof falls coming down the road, and the postmistress, Bertha, pulls up, horse and rider both sweating.

"A message," she gasps out, her long blonde hair sliding out from under her floppy sheepsweave hat, "from your husband. He says he'll be home within the week."

He's alive. Deep down, I knew he was, but I couldn't understand his silence, the long delay in hearing from him, and too often, reason dies a slow and painful death in the face of the unexplained. *But he's alive, and he's coming home.*

"He's sent a letter? But how did it arrive so—"

Bertha moves her hand through the air like a bird of prey, floating on unseen currents. "A mousesnatcher. Didn't know you could train them to do that, but that witch did. I'm sorry I opened it, Val, but I didn't know who it was for or even what it was!" She's breathing hard still, her round cheeks rosy with cold, but grinning hard. "He's coming back. He's on his way!"

Indeed, the letter says just that, paired with X's and O's at the bottom, but it is his hand.

He's alive.

Thank Woz, he's alive.

"Within the week, though?" my father rumbles. "How is this possible? If he reached the witch, he's ten days out, at least."

"She's got magic we've no knowledge of, Papa," I reply, hoping it's true. "He must not have turned around if she helped him send the letter." I scan the letter again. "He says to surrender the property under no circumstances. He's very clear on that point."

"We'll help you stand firm," Papa says, wrapping his thick arm around my shoulders, warming me inside and out. "And now we have it from his hand that those are his wishes."

"I just hope it'll be enough," I whisper, waving to the postmistress as she turns to leave.

CHAPTER SIXTEEN

Renault

Alya's asleep again. My arms ache from holding her, trying to shield her from the rocking of the carriage as the horses run. These wispy beasts nearly disappear when they put on speed, but it makes no difference to me what they are, as long as they can get me home. We left four days ago, before the mousesnatcher winged its way back to us, anxious to return now that the decision has been made and the Favor promised. I could see nothing as I signed the magical contract, but Alya squealed in delight, so something must have happened.

I emptied my stomach twice violently before we'd been in this massive, ornate carriage for an hour, so it seemed best to only eat sparingly since then. But this decision is not helping to keep my head from spinning. We stop only to relieve ourselves and stretch our legs, traveling through the night since no one in their right mind would try to rob a black carriage pulled by beasts such as these. What little sleep I've gotten has been against the rattling side, thankfully padded with sheep's wool under the violet velvet, so I'm not missing my pillow too much. But I stopped feeling my legs long ago with Alya on my lap. In vain, I try to shift her to the side, but she wakes, blinking groggily. Across from us, Lady Frost still sleeps soundly, curled under a brocaded quilt, her fingers twisted into the ribbon loops of the heavy covering, and the alternate driver is also out hard.

"Oh, is that Pont des Cerfs?" Alya asks, peeking out the curtains, and I shake my head.

"No, little bird, we're still a way off."

My voice rouses Lady Frost, and I smile apologetically as she stretches. "Did you sleep well, my lady?"

"Not in the slightest. I dreamed of earthshakers and giants passing by with jarring footsteps. And you?"

"I dozed off when I could."

Based on the little I can see through the curtains, dawn is also flexing her wings, about to take flight.

"We're almost there, Papa!" Alya is bouncing on the seat next to me, and when she whacks my leg in excitement, I can almost feel it through all the pins and pokes as my blood returns to my flesh. I rub my legs as I try to peer through the window again.

"I don't think so. Soon, though."

"The magic here knows me better, Papa. It's welcoming us home!" *If we have a home to come home to.* I've largely pushed the dark thought away as we traveled, but it arrests me now, making my insides clench hard. Alya's still bouncing, and my stomach revolts, sending me for the window in earnest, and to my astonishment, she's right. That's our neighbor, the widow Vallens, broom still poised to sweep, but frozen by the sight of the huge black carriage and the nightmare beasts that pull us along. I wave weakly, and she snaps out of it, returning the gesture. I stick my head out the window, letting the cold air refresh me and chase away the nerves...which is why I see the crowd before the rest of them.

"Stop the carriage!" I shout, pounding on the side, and I'm out and into the road, stumbling over my own boots on shaky legs before it's even stopped moving.

The two masses of people are shifting, restless, talking over one another in a cacophony worse than the chickens during a squabble. My gate sits firmly between the groups—those inside appear to be wielding makeshift weapons from my barn, as I recognize my stall shovel and my pitchfork with the third tine broken, and I know them all. They're my customers, they're the ones who sit near us in church, Jacob and his boys, even the postmistress.

Those outside seem to have raided their own barns, but it's a much smaller group, and I don't recognize many of them. Valerie stands at the front on our side, motionless and silent, staring down my pathetic cousin with her father at her back, his forge having supplied him better with weapons. *Valerie.* I realize I've forgotten about Alya entirely as I race toward my wife, leaping over the ditch near the fence and shoving my way past them all.

She cries out when she sees me, a base sound of elation as much as despair, and I've got her, I've got her, even though the rough gate is jammed into my ribs as I reach over it to embrace her, I've got her. I can't stop kissing her beautiful face, I can't stop petting her hair. I don't care who sees. This is what I've needed for days and days. This is where my home truly lies, whatever happens next.

"Are you all right? I'm so sorry, Val. I'm here now. We hurried best we could." She's just nodding, emotion stealing her words, her face tear-stained, but her smile brilliant. I put a foot on the gate and vault myself over to stand with her and address the crowd outside, but when I turn, they're not looking at me. Lady Frost has descended from the carriage and walks hand in hand with Alya toward us, and the people part before her as though she's entranced them. She looks every bit the enchantress despite how our carriage ride has disheveled and nearly destroyed me, her bearing regal, her black lace collar still stiff, and her dark hair coiled delicately on her head. I'd never say so aloud, but she might have used magic.

"A welcoming party for me? What a delight," she purrs, and a shiver races down even my spine—and I know she's not wicked. But they don't. My cousin Phillipe's face turns a particular shade of purple not unlike the interior of the carriage, and his mouth opens and closes like a fish. I don't really want to open the gate, but they all seem transfixed by her, so I just open it a crack, and she and Alya slip through. Even the crowd on our side ripples backward like they're afraid to touch her, like a drop of oil on water. "I can't wait to see where my cottage will be."

My cousin finds his voice then. "Your cottage, lady? There must be some mistake..."

"Why, yes. It's just been decided. In exchange for my tutelage for his extraordinary daughter, Renault has promised to build me a summer cabin here as a Favor, signed and sealed by contract. Would you like to inspect the paperwork?"

An older man next to him is glaring at Philippe, and he reaches out a hand. "I would, if you don't mind."

"Not at all. Gerard? The contract, please." Her driver hops down with the scroll, and there's some low murmuring and discussion over the paper before the man straightens.

"I'm sorry, Monsieur Cartier, but even I cannot act against a Favor. This gives her rights to the property in perpetuity, and it's clear that she intended it to have proximity to the child, so the laws of apprenticeship also apply. This matter is hereby closed." A raucous cheer from the crowd on our side goes up, and Valerie is looking at me slack-jawed with wonder in her gaze. I pull her close again—I may not be able to stop touching her for days—and kiss her forehead, then whisper, "I'll explain it all."

"I look forward to it," she whispers back as the crowd continues to roil around us. Someone's found a drum, and they're chanting and singing our victory as the angry ones outside the gate continue to argue and complain, throwing down their weapons in frustration. Then there are arms around my waist—someone's let the girls out of the house now that the threat of violence has passed, and I'm lifting Fayette's small form into my arms, laughing to see Margot's shining face, Clothilde squirming her way closer to me, too.

"Right this way, Lady Frost," I say, as I start across the yard, overflowing with friends and neighbors. I'll break ground on her small cabin tomorrow...or maybe the day after. She's assured me that there's no hurry, as she won't be back this way until the ground thaws. Until then, she means to send a journal back and forth with her mousesnatcher, Talon, to instruct us and help us ask less of the girl. To help her feel safe and whole, to let her see that we mean no threat by our requests, to help her know that our love is deep and wide. And it's all I wanted and more.

EPILOGUE

Renault

The front door is open, and the cherry blossoms sweep into the main room on the breeze when I come back in from milking Daisy, our new cow. I cover the bucket and set it next to the icebox for Valerie, pausing just a moment to kiss her. Without a word, I pick up the egg basket and hand it to Alya, who's currently holding court over a group of her cousins, who are embroidering napkins for Mireille, chattering together around the table. That was my lesson for the week—*talk less*. She gives me a put-upon look, but puts the basket handle over her arm and calls, "I'll be right back!"

It wasn't easy to give her that kind of trust—that's my business, the eggs. But we hadn't known she wanted the responsibility until we asked; we hadn't known that the dish task disgusted her, made her want to vomit. Of course, she broke a few eggs at first, but the look of pride on her face when she comes in from the cold is worth it.

The bell rings at the gate, and I head that way, relishing the feeling of not needing my heavy coat. It's Feline, Valerie's cousin, who gave me my first haircut here. "Come for my eggs or your girls?" I call, and she smiles.

"Neither. Does Alya have any mushrooms left? Luke's lungs are still poor, and I was hoping to give him a bit of help. Her mushrooms are better medicine than any tincture the doctor or Jeanette has come up with."

"True. I've felt the benefit of them myself," I say, opening the gate for her and beckoning her inside. "Let's go query the businesswoman herself."

Her steps slow as we near the house. "I just have to say what a change we all see in her. It's a credit to you."

A bit embarrassed, I run a hand through my hair. "She's shown us what she needs; we're just learning to follow her lead. I know it's all a bit...unorthodox. It's not the normal way of parents to follow their children, but it's our way."

Alya's coming toward us now, walking as fast as she safely can with my egg basket so full.

"Papa, here are your eggs. I'm back to embroidery," she says, ignoring Feline and thrusting the basket toward me.

"Hang on now, you've got a customer," I call after her, and she whips around, face concerned.

"Cousin Feline? Is Luke still sick?"

"Just a bit. Would you trade some yarn for your mushrooms?"

My girl shakes her blonde curls seriously. "I can't charge you. You're family. Let's see what I've got in stock."

Feline and I share a grin as Alya leads the way, clearly mentally pawing through her inventory already.

"And Madame Montagne comes back when?"

"A week's time. We'll be ready, I think. It'll be nice to have the rest of the girls home from school, now that the weather's nicer." I flex my hands without thinking about it...I've had quite a task, felling all the trees and processing them, but several men from the village came out to help in exchange for eggs and mushrooms, and I've managed to get the logs in place, and then the roof. Now we just need the interior items.

I'll be sure to tell Mireille about Alya's comment about family...such a change from the girl she was before our trip. Nothing's perfect, of course, and she still rages at us when she feels that we overstep or overcorrect, but we're getting there. A settled peace is more the norm than her tempests, and we all feel the benefit of it. It was worth whatever pain my muscles might be in from building the cabin.

Another ring of the bell has me turning back toward the gate. How she taught that damn bird to ring the bell, I'll never know, but Talon is sitting on the fence, watching me expectantly. We see him regularly, but we've had a letter from her just this week, so I didn't expect another so soon. I hurry to untie the message from the creature's leg, and he flies off immediately.

Dear Alya, Valerie and Renault,

I'm so sorry for the short notice, but I've been called away on a rescue mission of sorts for a dear friend, and I won't be able to come to you next week as I had anticipated. Alya, please continue with your exercises, and I will plan to come see you once my task is complete. Valerie and Renault, I apologize for the change of plans and hope you can forgive my absence.

Mireille

As if we wouldn't forgive her this small request. As if she hasn't helped us beyond measure, given us more than we could thank her for in a lifetime. I send up a silent prayer for her and her friend's protection, then head inside to give the family the news.

Thank you for reading this first installment of the Enchantress Chronicles! There's more to come from Mireille, Alya, and the family, but in the meantime, here's another strong heroine you might like in my fantasy romance series set in the same universe, many years later. Enjoy!

CHAPTER ONE

As Abelia stood on the platform, anticipating the vibration of the public light rail train's arrival, she never imagined it would be the last time.

It was a Wednesday, so those without train allowances were walking to work, streaming swiftly by like the waters of a brook, most babbling into their phones. She gripped her travel mug of coffee with one hand and stuffed the other deep into her uniform overalls to avoid human contact as people jostled around her. It made no sense to change at work, especially when one might sit in something sticky on the train.

Abbie loved watching the spaces between suburbs fly by. She loved the retro look of the seats and the conductors in their little hats, scanning people's phones for tickets. She didn't have a smartphone, so she dug around for her paper pass in her over-sized bag.

She loved riding in the opposite direction from most people. It took no time at all leaving the city in the morning compared to all those suckers riding into downtown, standing up like cattle. She rode from Tanner's Point through Binderville past Cottage Grove and Blakewood. The woods were lovely this time of year; spring was just arriving and the trees were all buds and possibilities. It made her want to sit by a creek and watch the fish jump. The window she peered out of seemed to stand still as the trees and buildings scrambled by. The recorded voice announced Beaver Landing, the last stop, and she hopped off.

Work was another story. It was hot underground—less like being in the sun and more like being in a sauna. A smelly sauna. The overalls were stifling but mandatory, their color indicating rank and their fabric soaking up unwanted chemicals from the air. They'd been specially designed, but they didn't work as well as their manufacturers claimed. And worst of all, being inside all day made her white, freckled skin even paler than it would naturally be. Then again, a waste reclamation plant was never going to be an attractive job.

"Start down on the end and work toward me," Abbie called to her team over the hissing air coming out of the vents. "We should be able to finish this load before lunch. Watch out for the aluminum, you missed some yesterday." As they dispersed, she went back to her clipboard and began looking over the day's quotas.

"Abbie?"

"Yo," she answered without looking up. Someone cleared his throat.

"Abelia Olivia Jayne Venenza Ribaldi Porchenzii?"

At this, she looked up slowly, her pencil still poised over the paper, cold realization coming down on her like a bucket of yesterday's wash water. Two people who looked to be related were smiling excitedly at her, then at each other. Their pale skin looked almost green under the fluorescent lights.

"Your Highness, thank the Woznick we found you! We need to speak with you."

Abbie set her mouth in a hard line. "I'm busy." She turned and walked back toward her office without another word. *Don't follow me, don't follow me...*

They followed.

"Your Highness," the woman began, but Abbie spun around, holding up a quelling hand.

"I left that title behind a long time ago. Please don't use it."

"What should we call you, then? Light of our hearts? Gracious one? Your worship?" The woman sounded completely serious. Abbie tried not to roll her eyes.

"Just Abbie is fine," she said, her gaze returning to her clipboard.

"That won't do," whispered the woman to the man. She snapped her fingers. "We'll call you sister, then?"

"Are you in a cult? Because I have no interest in cults. Coffee is my religion."

The man removed his hat. "Perhaps Your Highness would like to discuss this somewhere more private?"

Abbie forced herself to smile politely for the sake of a few curious onlookers. Hanging up her clipboard on the wall, she badged them into the corridor of offices where things smelled a bit better and led them to hers, closing the door behind them.

"Please allow me to introduce ourselves," said the man. "I am Rubald Jerrinson, and this is my favorite wife, Rutha." He pronounced it *"Root-ah,"* a name Abbie had only heard once before in her 21 years. He cleared his throat nervously as she paged through the stack of papers in her inbox. "We're on a diplomatic mission from Orangiers," he continued, "a mission of the gravest importance."

No, it couldn't be. He wouldn't. It's been years since I left. Just stay frosty.

Abbie allowed her eyebrows to lift in faux surprise. "You've come a long way, then."

"Yes, Highness."

"I thought we'd agreed on *sister*, Mr. Jerrinson," Abbie said, though they'd agreed on no such thing. She heaved a sigh. "I don't want these people knowing who I...was."

In truth, Gardenia's capital city was a popular spot for erstwhile princes and princesses of all sorts, and she knew several, though none from countries as large and powerful as Brevspor. Most were perpetual philosophy majors at the university, living off trust funds. By working at the plant, she had been able to keep her identity under wraps. Until now.

"Yes, apologies, erm, *sister*," Rubald said with a nervous little cough. "We've been sent to bring you to fulfill your contractual obligation to marry His Royal Highness, Second Son of Orangiers, Prince Edward Kenneth Keith Francis Benson Broward. We must leave as soon as possible."

Abbie stood up and walked to the corner of her office where a mini-fridge and a coffeepot lived. She pulled out a pink toaster pastry, her go-to when-I'm-stressed-out food, and poured herself another cup of coffee. She sat back down at her desk without offering the two emissaries anything. They wouldn't be staying long enough to enjoy it if she had her way.

"That contract became void when I renounced my title and position in line to the throne," she said through her first enormous bite of pastry. Despite her best efforts, her heartrate was starting to climb.

The couple smiled at each other knowingly, and Rutha pulled a thin stack of papers out of a satchel Abbie hadn't noticed she was carrying. "This copy of the contract says otherwise," the woman said. "You can read it yourself if you'd like, Your Ma—ah, sister. We've just highlighted the salient conditions there, under 'bridal conditions'...your royal status isn't one of them, and you never formally renounced your title. Please remember that international marriage contracts are enforceable in any country on the continent or across the Sparkling Sea, so your presence in a foreign country is no obstacle. We have spoken to the leaders of Gardenia privately, and they've agreed to extradite you to Orangiers if necessary."

A vise tightened in Abbie's chest, her fear rising fast in a hot, panicky wave. "I need some time to look over this contract," she said, her voice surprisingly even to her own ears. She stood up and walked to the door. "Would you both please come back tomorrow, say around ten, when we can discuss this further?" Her thoughts were already racing ahead to her best friend Lauren with her law degree, to a large glass of wine, and to the "go bag" with a stack of new identities in a train station locker she'd been renting for five years. Anything but the terrifying specter of a thousand-person church wedding and a gold circlet back on her head.

"There's something else, sister." Rubald paused. His pale face was grave. "It's your father." Did she want to hear this? After stealing away in the night without even saying goodbye? Her tenderhearted father would've been heartbroken to say the least...

Abbie crossed to the desk and sat back down, curiosity getting the better of her.

"He's written you a letter. I have it here." She reached out and took the large manila envelope Rubald offered. Her father's wax seal straddled the flap, but her name was written in a shaky hand she didn't recognize. She broke the seal quickly and removed the fine linen sheet. It was shorter than she'd expected.

Dearest Abbie,

You are missed more than you can imagine. Things are not going well here, and your help is needed. I am ill. The people do not wish your brother to ascend to the throne. Brevspor has been a matriarchy for sixteen generations, and the people do not accept the way things are now. They tolerated my leadership after your mother passed away, knowing that you were too young to shoulder such responsibility, but no more.

They have petitioned me to enforce your marriage contract. Under your joint leadership with Edward, they believe Brevspor would flourish, and of course, I agree. Brevspor would come under control of Orangiers as a territory with you as its steward, and they would have a Porchenzii queen they trust once more.

There is more. Other ruling powers know what a powerful alliance this would be, and are working swiftly to prevent it. You are in danger where you are. I'm sorry for this, but thought it better that you know.

Come say goodbye to me, my darling daughter, and take your rightful place...for all our sakes.

Love,

Paul Daniel Trevor Washington Frakes Porchenzii...aka Dad

All the royal training in the world wasn't enough to keep her emotions under control. Five years of silence, broken with such news. She couldn't stop the tears that blurred her vision, and she wiped at them with angry swipes. She reread the first line over and over: *You are missed more than you can imagine.* It was more loving and gracious than she deserved after the way she'd treated him, her most precious ally.

"What kind of illness is it?" she asked quietly, smoothing the pristine letter against her cluttered desktop.

Mr. Jerrinson shrugged, his expression guileless. "I'm sorry, Highness, I don't know." She didn't bother correcting him. Suddenly, another line caught her eye. She wiped the snot escaping her nose on her sleeve and asked, "What does this mean, 'your joint leadership'? Is Edward now first in line for the throne as Second Son?"

Rubald nodded. "The First Son, Lincoln Atticus Jonathan Norris Bryant Broward, tried to seize power before his father announced his intention to step down. He's been deemed unfit to rule and currently sits in exile in Op'ho'lonia. He mounts an army there even now to attempt another coup—that is, until his brother marries and gains the advantage of your territory's forces, at which point he'll be..."

"Irrelevant," she finished. *Irrelevant, just like this letter.* If she went back now, it would all have been for nothing. Discomfort turned her stomach, but she refused to let it now. She might not be a royal anymore, but she knew how to comport herself. Abbie wiped her face again, the tears still refusing to stop. Rutha offered her an embroidered handkerchief, which she gratefully took.

"Damn it," she whispered. "Damn it all to Jersey."

"Majesty," Rutha said quietly, "regarding the danger your father spoke of, we believe you should plan to leave here as soon as possible."

"No," she replied, blowing her nose. She stared them down through reddened eyes that matched her hair. "You may leave now."

Twin expressions of shock appeared on the couple's faces, but Rubald found his voice first. "Majesty, we both feel—"

Abbie rose to her feet and slammed her palms down on the desk, scattering papers and the pastry wrapper to the floor. "I do not care what you feel, what you think, or what you want," she enunciated slowly and clearly. "I have left that life behind permanently. I will *never* return to a royal life. You are welcome to try to extradite me if you dare."

"Oh my," Rutha muttered, and Rubald just shook his head. They stared at her, Rubald's face turning a mottled red, but didn't move until she cleared her throat.

"Let me be more clear. Get. out."

<u>Start this complete, whimsical, fairy-tale romance series to-day!</u>[1]

---

1. https://readerlinks.com/l/3971068

Acknowledgments

I call myself an indie author because while independent, I certainly don't do it all myself! Deepest gratitude goes to:

- my sensitivity reader, J.R. Hart
- my friend and proofreader, Liz Schandorff
- my copyeditor, Your Publishing BFF, Dayna
- my writing Discord group, who never fails to encourage me to make art
- my kids, who are amazing in every way, even when the walls are covered in peanut butter
- and of course, my soulmate, my CFO, and the love of my life.

Connect with Fiona!

Thanks so much for taking the time to sample my work. I hope you enjoyed reading it even more than I enjoyed writing it, though I doubt that's possible. Being an author is a dream come true, and getting to share my books with delightful, thoughtful readers like you just adds to the sweetness. Drop me a line and let me know what you thought or leave a review on Goodreads, Storygraph, TikTok, or wherever you like!

Sign up for my newsletter for freebies, deleted scenes, book reviews, and insight into my writing process at https://www.subscribepage.com/becareful.

On Facebook as @authorfionawest[1]

On Instagram as @fionawestauthor[2]

On Goodreads as Fiona West[3]

Or email me at fiona@fionawest.net. I love talking to fans!

---

1. https://web.facebook.com/authorfionawest/

2. https://www.instagram.com/fionawestauthor/

3. https://www.goodreads.com/author/show/18433825.Fiona_West

9 781952 172502